The Warlock's Bride

Silveri Sisters
Book 2

R. L. Medina

For my husband. The calm to my chaos.

List of Characters
People (and animals) of Zamerra

Signora Gloria Silveri (Mama)

The matriarch of the Silveri family. She is a seer who arrived in Zamerra with her five daughters and no husband. Meddlesome at times, she will do anything for her girls.

Alessia Silveri

The oldest of the Silveri daughters. Unlike her sisters, she has no magic, but she is the only one who can hear the enchanted villa speak. She is married to Massimo Gallo, a half-fae count, making her the Contessa of Zamerra and surrounding region.

Liliana Silveri

The second oldest of the Silveri daughters. Her magic skill is with brewing potions and performing spells.

Pamina Silveri

The third oldest and middle child of the Silveri family. She has baking magic and also makes the best, magical caffé.

Serafina Silveri (Fina)

The fourth daughter in the Silveri family. She can talk to and command animals.

Fiorella Silveri (Ella)

The youngest Silveri sister. She has plant and earth magic which she struggles to control at times.

Count Massimo Gallo

The half-fae count who would rather sit in his favorite chair with a book than make public speeches. He falls in love with the oldest Silveri sister, Alessia.

Dante Lazzaro

Massimo's best friend and skilled warlock. He makes and sells his own potions. He also drives Liliana crazy.

Ometta

Dante's owl familiar.

Signora Gavella

Dante's mentor and friend. She runs a potion shop in the city and gifts him a special love potion.

Salvatore Rossi

The Silveri's neighbor and friend. He is married to Adriano, a faun, and is the oldest of the Rossi brothers.

Adriano Rossi

Salvatore's faun husband. An introvert, he prefers to stay home and throw dinner parties. Heir to an enormous fortune, he and his husband are able to enjoy their quiet life just outside of Zamerra.

Signora Donatella

A wealthy city woman who buys potions from Dante.

Signor Marcello

Liliana's rival. He runs the town's oldest apothecary and likes to spread rumors about Liliana's witchiness.

Other characters:

Rafaelo Rossi

The second oldest Rossi brother. He is quiet and reserved, taking after his father. He will inherit the Rossi goat and horse farm.

Angelo Rossi

The third oldest Rossi brother. An extrovert, he is often the spokesman for his family and has a fondness for Serafina Silveri.

Marco Rossi

The youngest of the Rossi family. He helps his brothers on their farm.

Signor Covelli

The town baker. He owns the bakery next to Dante's potion shop.

Bruno

The Silveri's house elf.

Franny

Alessia and Masssimo's house elf.

Lucia

Massimo's spoiled cat.

Gio

The scrappy little dog that has become a part of the cat gang that lives in the Silveri's yard.

Fabrizio

The Silveri's old horse.

Chapter 1

Witch's Brew

Liliana

A cool breeze drifted in from the kitchen window, bringing with it the smell of autumn. Crisp leaves and an earthy scent briefly masked the burnt fungus and rotten berry smell. Briefly.

Liliana looked down at the bubbling black mixture in the cauldron as she stirred. Another hour or so and it would be ready to cool and pour into the vials she had readied on the table. Her tight curls clung to her face in the heat of the kitchen. Even with the outside air coming from the window and open door, the room felt stuffy.

The pantry burst open behind her. She stopped stirring and turned to see Bruno, their little house elf, barrel out with an angry scowl.

"How did you get out? You can't reach the knob," Liliana asked.

She glanced up at the wooden rafters. Though she couldn't sense its magic, she suspected the villa had a part in Bruno's escape. Her older sister had always suspected their villa was enchanted.

Bruno shouted something in elvish to Liliana, covered his nose with his hand, and stomped out the back door. He'd get her back for shutting him in his room, she was sure, but she didn't have a choice. It was impossible to work with the little elf loose. He liked to 'help' her by adding his own ingredients to her mixtures.

Making potions and salves was tricky. One wrong ingredient or too much of her magic could turn a healing tonic into a deadly one. That would be just what they needed—to kill off some of the townsfolk.

Even with her older sister, Alessia, married to the count (a fae count at that) the people of Zamerra were still wary of Liliana and her four younger sisters. The Silveri girls were witches, after all.

"Do you have to do that here?" a voice called from the open door.

Liliana turned to see her sister Serafina. "Where else am I supposed to do this?"

Serafina made a sour face. "It smells like something died in here. How are we supposed to eat in here now? Does Pamina know you're brewing? Does Mama know?"

Irritation filled Liliana at her younger sister's pestering. She turned her back to her and kept stirring, trying her best to ignore her. With Alessia gone and married, Liliana was the oldest sister in the villa now, and she was supposed to set a good example for the younger girls.

Flinging the sticky, smelly goop at Serafina would not be setting a good example. Although the thought of doing it made Liliana smile.

"*Santo cielo!* What is that smell?" Pamina, the third oldest, asked as she appeared in the doorway with a sack of groceries.

Their youngest sister, Fiorella, walked in behind her with another sack. Her nose scrunched up in disgust.

"It's not that bad," Liliana said, returning to stirring.

Serafina snorted behind her. "It smells like the backside of a dirty, sick boar."

"Fina!" Pamina admonished their sister.

Liliana paused to let the goo settle and turned back to her sisters. "Charming as always, Fina."

Serafina stuck her tongue out at Liliana, acting more like Fiorella's ten years than the fifteen years she was.

Pamina and Fiorella set down the groceries on the wooden countertop near the sink. Bruno came running inside to see what they'd bought. He cast a disdainful look at Liliana before climbing the stool to reach the counter.

"How much longer until it's done? I wanted to get started on the minestrone for supper," Pamina said, her voice muffled as she held a cloth up to her nose.

"What are you brewing?" Fiorella asked, braving a step closer to peek.

"Sleeping tonic. It has about an hour or more." Liliana answered.

"No one is going to want to drink that. Not if it tastes as bad as it smells," Serafina gave her unwanted opinion.

Something she enjoyed doing too often.

Liliana shot her a look. "One more smart comment and you'll get the first taste." She waved the wooden spoon at her in warning.

Serafina's nostrils flared, her near black eyes flashing with anger.

"Where is Mama?" Fiorella asked, breaking the tension in the kitchen.

They all looked to Liliana. Liliana frowned. She remembered their mother telling her something before she left, but she couldn't remember what she'd said. When she was in the middle of her work, she couldn't focus on anything else.

Outside, the cats and Gio, the little dog that followed them around, started yowling and barking, alerting them to a visitor. Liliana returned to her work while Serafina and Fiorella ran outside to see who was at their gate.

Pamina stayed behind, unloading their purchases while Bruno waited eagerly to see if they'd brought him anything. He held his little, pointed red hat in his hands and hopped from one slippered foot to the other.

"Oh, did you know that a new shop is opening in town?" Pamina asked as she handed Bruno a copper coin.

The little elf took it, jumped down to the stool then the floor, and headed for the pantry, where he stashed all his treasures.

"It's where Signora Prato's birdhouse shop used to be," Pamina continued as she put a small sack of sugar inside the wooden cupboard.

A snort escaped Liliana. "I'm surprised her shop lasted as long as it did. Who needs birdhouses?"

Pamina paused and glanced over her shoulder to Liliana. "Well, birds, I imagine. Anyways, we didn't get a good look from the window, but it looks like it's going to be some type of apothecary."

Liliana frowned. "An apothecary? But we already have one."

Pamina shrugged. A mahogany curl fell from her loose bun as she turned to face Liliana. "I wouldn't worry too much about it. Everyone knows your tonics are the best. Even Signor Marcello would agree."

Liliana grunted in response. The town's pharmacist, Signor Marcello, was her biggest rival. Not only was he pig-headed and rude, but he actively spread rumors that her tonics were nothing but water and mud that didn't work.

Despite his gossip, the townsfolk knew her stuff was real. She had her magic, but he still had the respect of the town.

"*Santo Cielo!* Liliana, that brew is strong," Mama's voice interrupted her thoughts.

Their mother entered the kitchen with Serafina and Fiorella by her side. The cats and little Gio swarmed around their ankles, mewling and whimpering for Serafina's attention. Unlike Liliana, Serafina's magic was talking to animals. Wherever she went, critters hovered near her.

She smiled smugly at Liliana. "I told you she wouldn't like your brew."

"Brat," Liliana muttered.

Serafina's tan face reddened, and her mouth opened to protest, but their mother stepped in with a hand raised to silence her.

"Once it's finished, we'll light some candles and hang some flowers. Now, go finish up your chores, girls. I have some exciting news to share," Mama said with a clap of her hands.

Pamina and Liliana exchanged looks. What was their mother up to now?

* * *

Liliana filled the last vial and gave Pamina a nod to bring the crate over. She'd let the vials cool a little bit more before she corked them, but she wanted to get them off the table before any accidents happened.

"I'll help!" Fiorella exclaimed, joining Liliana.

Pamina set the wooden crate on the table beside the tonics. Fiorella grabbed a vial in each hand and put them in the crate. The glass clinked together.

Liliana sucked in a breath. "Careful!"

Fiorella gave her a sheepish look as she reached for another vial. This time, using the cloth Pamina brought to cushion it, she set it next the others.

Outside, wind whistled through the trees, rustling the leaves.

Fiorella paused with a frown.

"What?" Liliana asked.

Her sister shook her head and pushed her long chestnut hair over her shoulder. "Nothing. I thought... I thought I heard someone talking."

"Is it the villa? Can you hear it like Alessia can?" Pamina asked carefully, turning to them with a knife and carrot in her hands.

"No. It must have been the wind. I don't hear it now," Fiorella said, returning to the vials.

Liliana shared a look with Pamina. Living up the mountain, they were surrounded by the forest and when she was younger, Fiorella would wander among the trees, claiming the voices called her.

If she was hearing voices again that was a bad sign. They would need to talk to Mama about another spell to smother her power.

Fiorella's earth and plant magic was still developing, but already it had proven to be stronger than everyone else's and the most volatile. Anything plant, flower, vegetable, or fruit that she touched would take on strange properties. Sometimes deadly.

"Do you need help with the soup? I can chop," Fiorella asked Pamina, oblivious to her older sister's silent exchange.

Pamina hesitated. Her light brown eyes darted to Liliana.

"I'll wear the gloves," Fiorella added quickly, giving Pamina a hopeful look.

Pamina smiled at her and motioned her over to the counter. "Alright."

"Hold on. Let me check them first," Liliana said as she

moved the crate off the table and placed it in the corner of the kitchen.

Fiorella brought the silk gloves to her, the green matching her eyes. They'd been a gift from their sister Alessia and her husband to help control Fiorella's magic touch.

"Do you think I'll have to wear them forever?" Fiorella asked, her voice growing small.

Pamina gave her a pitying look. Liliana held the enchanted gloves in her hand and met Fiorella's eyes.

"Until you have better control of your magic, Ella. You know that," Liliana answered firmly.

Closing her eyes, Liliana said a quick chant, making sure the gloves were ready to block Fiorella's power. An icy surge of magic filled her briefly before dissipating. Finished, she handed the gloves back to her sister.

Fiorella took them with a pout. "It's not fair. I didn't have to wear them before. I've been practicing more than ever but it's only gotten worse. Why?"

"Maybe it's a sign that your nearing your womanhood," Pamina answered mid-chop.

Both Fiorella and Liliana made a face. Before either could respond, Serafina appeared through the open doorway.

"All done! When's supper?" she asked, stomping her boots on the little rug.

Her trousers were covered with hay and dirt and a line of something that Liliana hoped was just mud streaked her tan freckled face. Mama walked up behind her, somehow looking regal in her brown canvas gardening pants and cotton shirt.

"I just started," Pamina answered, returning to her chopping.

Serafina sighed dramatically, stepping out of her boots before entering the kitchen. "Can't you use a spell to make the soup cook faster?" she directed her question to Liliana.

Mama clucked her tongue, closing the back door behind them. "No. Spells are not to be used for such trivial things, *amore*." She tucked one of Serafina's fallen auburn curls back into her headwrap.

"Why not? If I could do spells like that, I wouldn't have to do so many chores," Serafina argued.

Mama's dark eyebrow arched at her in warning.

"And then you'd be lazy and magic dependent," Liliana said with a snort.

"No, I wouldn't," Serafina shot back.

"Enough. Fiorella, do you want to grab some flowers to hang up?" Mama asked, turning to the youngest Silveri sister.

Fiorella stopped chopping and nodded. She peeled off her gloves and set them on the counter.

"Oh, before you go, I have some news. I wanted to wait until supper, but it's just too exciting," Mama said, clapping her hands together.

"What is it?" both Serafina and Fiorella asked in unison.

Mama grinned. "Zamerra is holding its first Hallow's Eve masquerade!"

Gasps and excited squeals followed, making Liliana wince. Bruno, who'd stuck his head out of the pantry to listen, quickly disappeared, hands covering his pointed ears.

"A masquerade? How exciting!" Pamina gushed, wiping her hands on her apron that hugged her curvy hips.

"Where did you hear this?" Liliana asked, her voice rising above the other's chatter.

Mama met her gaze. "I went to visit Alessia today and we started talking about Hallow's Eve coming up and how wary the town is of it. We thought a masquerade would be perfect to show them there's nothing to be afraid of. Many of the larger towns and cities do it."

A harsh laugh escaped Liliana. "And who better to host it

than the Zamerra witches. As if we're not already an oddity here. Let's gather everyone together when magic is at its most volatile so they can gawk at us."

Her mother sighed heavily and gave her a weary look. "You don't give them a chance, Liliana. Not everyone in town is our enemy. We can't let the past hold us back from making a better future."

Liliana shook her head. How was it so easy for her mother and sisters to forget the town's prejudices against them? The cruel whispers and stares.

"This is a bad idea, Mama. They know about Pamina's magic and mine, but what if they discover Serafina and Fiorella's? Hallow's Eve is not the right time for this, Mama. It's too dangerous."

"There will be safeguards in place," Mama answered, shrugging off Liliana's concern.

She wanted to disagree but held her tongue. There would be no point. It was an argument she and her mother continuously had. Let her mother and sisters believe what they wanted about the masquerade, she would make sure her family was protected.

They couldn't trust anyone outside themselves.

"If you're so opposed to it, don't come. You'll just spoil it for everyone anyway with your sourness," Serafina said.

"Fina! Don't say that," Pamina rushed to Liliana's defense.

"Go help Fiorella with the flowers. Now," Mama said sternly, pointing the two girls outside.

She turned to Pamina and Liliana, her dark eyes studying them calmly. "Alessia has asked for our help with this, and I expect the both of you to do your part. Things are changing in Zamerra. Magic isn't as...unaccepted as it used to be. This is a good thing."

Liliana fought the urge to roll her eyes. She wanted to argue but held her tongue. There would be no point. Let her mother and sisters believe what they wanted about the masquerade, she would make sure her family was protected.

She glanced at the vials in the corner. They were going to need more than sleeping tonic.

Chapter 2

Warlock's Potion

Dante

"Signor Lazzaro!" A feminine voice called behind Dante.

He stopped on the street and turned to see Signora Donatella heading for him with a determined look. He pasted on a friendly smile and took his hat off to greet her with an inward groan.

"Signora. How are you and Signor Donatella?"

She frowned at the mention of her husband and waved away his question. "Fine. Fine. I've been trying to call on you, but you never seem to be at home."

"Yes, well, I apologize, but I've been quite busy running errands and preparing for my leave."

Her eyes narrowed. "Strange. I haven't seen you around the shops either."

Dante's smile tightened. Was the woman tracking his every move?

"Oh, I've been traveling out of the city. Can't always find what I need here, you see."

Dante met her sharp gaze. They both knew he was lying,

11

and they both knew why. Ever since he'd sold her a few bottles of skin rejuvenation, she'd been hounding him for a house 'call' and showing up at every turn. She was an attractive woman, but Dante had no interest in starting an affair with her nor anyone else in the city.

The face of a certain brown-eyed witch flashed in his mind. Everything he wanted was waiting for him in Zamerra.

"Well, I do hope to call on you before you leave, Signore. Delle Rose won't be the same without you," Signora Donatella's sugary voice interrupted his thoughts.

She brushed a hand suggestively across his chest, holding his gaze.

"There are plenty of other warlocks and witches in the city. I'm sure they'll be able to supply all your needs," Dante replied.

Carnal or otherwise.

She huffed. "The ones who make house calls aren't nearly as... talented as you."

"There are the shops then," Dante said, nodding in the direction of one of the potions shop he'd been heading for.

The woman's lip curled. "As if I'd be caught stepping foot into one of *those places.*"

Normally, Dante would hold his tongue. Play the part of the charming warlock everyone knew him to be. But this was his last day in the city. The last time he had to put up with their snide remarks about magic and those who used it.

"How unfortunate," he said, leaning in toward her, "that last skin potion I made for you won't last for long. In fact, it looks as if it's already starting to wear off. I'd say you have about a week. At most. Then you'll have to find another way to hide your crowsfeet, Signora."

She gasped, a hand jumping to her face. Dante turned away from her and started walking, smiling at the angry sputter that echoed behind him.

An invisible bell jingled as he entered Signora Gavella's potion shop. The elderly witch looked up from the counter and gave him a wide smile.

"Ahh. There's my favorite warlock," she crooned.

Dante gave her a mock look of worry. "Careful! The others might hear you."

Ignoring him, the wizened woman hobbled toward him and gave him a tight hug that belied her frail appearance. Her frizzy gray hair tickled him as she nestled her face into his side, her head barely reaching his chest.

"I'm going to miss you so, *amore*. Promise you'll write as soon as your settled?"

She pulled away, wiping her eyes with the back of her hand.

A lump grew in Dante's throat. He cleared it and squeezed her lightly on the shoulder. "Promise. Now, no more tears, Signora. If you cry, I cry and I'm an ugly crier."

The witch scoffed. "Nonsense. You couldn't make yourself ugly even if you wanted to. I'm sure all your admirers would agree with me. I hope you've let them all down gently. The poor dears."

"All my admirers? Signora, you make me sound like such a rake. It hasn't been that many."

She gave him a flat look.

"Well, I'm a changed man now. No more parties and scandals. And you're the only one I'll miss." Dante flashed her a smile. Though his tone was teasing, he meant every word.

The witch snorted and motioned him over to the counter.

Dante followed, glancing around the quiet little shop. All her potions were lovingly displayed on the shelves behind enchanted glass. The distinct smell of roses and candlewax filled the room. He would miss coming there. Signora Gavella had become somewhat of a mentor to Dante. More a mother to him than his own mother had been.

"This is for you. A going away gift, if you will," the witch said, pulling out a small vial of black liquid.

Dante accepted her gift and held it up to his eyes. "What is it?"

Her grin widened. "A love potion."

Dante chuckled and started to hand it back to her. "Thank you, Signora, but I don't need it. I've never had trouble in that... particular area."

She pushed the vial back toward him. "Not for stamina, you fool. Love is more than a tussle in the sheets. Or carriage," she added with a faraway look.

A startled cough escaped Dante, making the witch frown.

"Listen to me, *amore*. There's more to life than magic."

Dante grunted, holding back the argument on his tongue.

The witch gave him a sad smile. "You may fool the others, but you can't fool me. You're not as happy with being alone as you pretend. Take it. Drink it. It will reveal your true match."

"Thank you," Dante said, pushing the vial deep into his pocket.

A love potion. What did that even mean? Magic couldn't make someone fall in love. Not permanently, anyway. Though Dante was no expert in the matter.

Pushing away the thoughts, he smiled at the witch. "Are the other potions ready?"

She nodded. "All set. If you need more, write me and I'll send them. Anything you need and don't be a stranger. I hope this won't be the last I see of you."

"Of course not, Signora. Can't get rid of me that easily."

"Oh, I've also got your honey cakes ready. Let me wrap them up for you," Signora Gavella said, turning away.

Dante grinned at her words. "And that's why you're the only woman I'll miss."

* * *

Dante stood in the middle of his villa and sighed. Memories, both good and bad, flooded his mind as his gaze swept the room. Blood red carpet, forest green walls, and black and gold accents everywhere. It was moody, dark, extravagant, and totally at odds with his usual sunny disposition.

He loved it.

A wave of sadness struck him as he realized he could no longer call the place home. The new owners, a non-magical family, would no doubt make it their own. Another respectable villa that looked identical to all the others on the street.

How boring.

Despite his sorrow at leaving, Dante was also excited. The change of address had been a long time coming. With his best friend, Massimo, now a count and living in marital bliss, there wasn't much keeping him in Borgo Delle Rose.

He'd spent nearly fifteen years there, but it had never truly felt like home. Signora Gavella's words echoed in his mind. *You're not as happy with being alone as you pretend.*

Maybe she was right. The parties he used to love had grown dull. Even flirting and romance had lost their excitement. What had changed?

Shaking himself out of his thoughts, Dante walked over to the black iron chest and unlocked it with a quick spell. He pulled out the small vial the witch had given him and looked at it once more.

Love potion.

Perhaps he could sell it to one of the townsfolk in Zamerra. He certainly wasn't going to waste it on himself. Placing it carefully beside all his other potions, salves, and ingredients, he turned to look at the small wooden box of potions he'd bought from Signora Gavella. A mixture of healing and beauty tonics. Perfect to sell in his apothecary.

With Massimo's fae blood and his new bride, Alessia, being a witch, Dante hoped magic would be more accepted in the mountains. Even so, he didn't want to use the term *potion shop* just in case.

Give the townsfolk a chance to warm up to him. Though, if he was being honest, he didn't much care about their opinion of him. There was only one woman in particular that he hoped to impress.

Liliana Silveri. Alessia's sister.

Her face flashed before him. Sharp, brown eyes framed with long dark lashes, glossy black curls, and full lips. She was stunning. Even when she was glaring at him.

The few interactions they'd had, he'd attempted to charm her, but everything that usually worked on other women didn't work on her.

She was smart and her quick tongue was a match for his own. Despite his best efforts to get to know her, she'd made it clear she was not interested in him. There had to be a reason she'd built such a high wall around herself, and Dante was determined to find out what it was.

Golden streaks of waning sunlight streamed in from his large windows. Soon it would be nightfall and Ometta, his owl familiar, would be ready to hunt. The move to the mountains would be good for her too. There would be much more forest and wilderness for her to explore.

The bells of a wagon cart sounded from outside, interrupting his thoughts. Dante walked to his front door and opened it to see a mail carrier heading toward his villa. He gave the man a friendly wave as he came to a stop.

"Good evening, Signor Lazzaro. I have a letter for you," the young man said, reaching into his satchel.

"Thank you," Dante replied as he took the outstretched letter.

He watched as the mail carrier took off, his wagon cart nearly empty of packages. Glancing down at the letter in his hand, Dante's eyebrows arched in surprise.

It was from Zamerra, from his friend Massimo. He opened it eagerly and skimmed over the greetings and updates.

A masquerade.

Massimo and his bride were hosting their very first masquerade. The first one in Zamerra. It had to be her idea. Dante couldn't imagine Massimo would want to put on such a thing. Though he couldn't imagine Alessia as the fancy masquerade type either.

Very curious.

Tucking the letter into his pocket, he glanced around the quiet, cobblestoned street. Dark iron lampposts lined the road. The brick and stone villas were clustered together, window planters filled with dying flowers and brown leaves.

Cold, autumn air swirled around Dante as he took it all in. The closer they were to Hallow's Eve, the stronger the pull of magic was. Dante hoped to be completely settled with his shop all set up before then. That would give him time to work on some new potions and spells to have ready in time.

He didn't know what to expect in Zamerra, but if people were as superstitious there as they were in the city, he wanted to have enough talismans to go around. Though he doubted there were many spirits looking to cross over in the little mountain town. They were usually drawn to bigger crowds.

Dismissing the thought, Dante turned to go back inside. He patted the letter in his pocket with growing excitement. A masquerade could be fun. *I'll need a new suit.*

As soon as he stepped inside, Ometta flew at him, her shiny

black wings flapping gracefully. Her bright yellow eyes met his. She was ready to hunt.

Dante opened the door wider to let the giant owl out. She glided out the front door without a glance back. Dante watched her disappear before closing the door. He'd leave his bedroom window open for when she was ready to return.

Growing weary, Dante sank into his armchair and lit the candle on the side table. He turned over the letter in his hand. As if it would reveal more details the longer he stared.

Would Liliana be there? The memory of their last encounter flashed before him. He'd come on too strong and she'd given him a verbal lashing that made his ears burn... among other things.

A snort escaped him, sounding loud in the quiet. Dante hated the silence. It was when he found himself alone in the quiet that the voices of the past echoed loudest. Namely, his father's.

Why do you waste your life with frivolous magic? You could have been so much more. You are a disappointment.

No matter what he did with his magic, it would never be good enough. He would never be good enough. His father was long gone now, but his words still lingered.

Dante stood up and turned on his phonograph. Soft music filled his villa, silencing the voices and memories.

Chapter 3

An Unpleasant Surprise

Liliana

L iliana sat at her sister's long kitchen table and sipped her caffé by the cozy fire. Strings of garlic hung from the wooden rafters, their sharp scent clashing with the freshly brewed caffé and sugary treats Pamina had brought.

They were gathered together to discuss the upcoming masquerade. The first official masquerade ever held in their little mountain town and, hopefully, the last. Franny, Alessia's little house elf, sat atop the wooden table beside them, her pointed red hat placed next to her.

While the others mulled over tablecloths, décor, and menu items, Liliana sat and listened. Alessia hadn't asked for her opinion yet, which was probably for the best. Liliana doubted they wanted to hear what she thought.

A masquerade. It was stupid. A waste of time. Their mother no doubt had a hand in convincing Alessia and Massimo into this, but why?

Liliana had a dark suspicion it had to do with matchmaking more than easing the townsfolk's fear of Hallow's Eve. After her scheming to push Alessia and Massimo together, her focus had turned to Liliana.

Mama thought she was so subtle, but Liliana was no fool.

Their mother was seer and the vision she had shared of Liliana's supposedly future child was a sore subject between them. One that Liliana had refused to entertain.

Children. Matchmaking. Marriage.

She wanted no part in it.

The warm liquid filled Liliana, settling her nerves. *Pamina's special brew.* Her sister's magic was with food and drink. Particularly, sweets that brought healing and peace. Unlike Liliana, Pamina didn't have to worry about accidentally poisoning anyone with *her* magic.

"You're quiet," Alessia finally addressed her.

"Hmm," Liliana returned.

She met her sister's gaze and held it, speaking volumes with her silence. As the oldest Silveri sisters, she and Alessia had a special bond. They were best friends. Or had been until Alessia had gone and married the fae count. At least they had built a villa right up the road. Liliana couldn't stand the thought of living far from any of her sisters.

Alessia frowned. "What is it? I know dances and parties aren't usually something you enjoy, but don't you think the townsfolk deserve a celebration? Something to look forward to before harvest time? Everyone has been working so hard."

"Does it even matter what I think?"

"Of course, it does." Alessia's brown eyes narrowed. Like Liliana, she had inherited their mother's black curls, dark eyes and bronze skin, but that was where the similarities ended.

Alessia and Pamina were the nicer sisters. Liliana was stony. So, she was told.

Headstrong. Standoffish. Sharp.

"Don't be such a sour puss," Serafina piped in with a mouthful of cannoli.

Liliana ignored her, staring down at her berry-stained fingers curled around her steaming mug. A wave of heat came from the fire blazing in the stone hearth behind her.

"Well, I think a masquerade is a lovely idea!" Pamina broke the tension with a sigh and clap of her hands.

Liliana snorted. "Well, of course you do. You love cooking and baking."

"You wouldn't have to do much, Liliana. I'm sure we could manage without you," Alessia said softly.

Liliana's chest tightened. She knew her sister meant well, but she couldn't help but feel the sting of her words. *We can manage without you.*

"Oh, please. She's just cranky because she knows a certain gorgeous warlock will be invited," Serafina said with a smug smirk.

Liliana's hand tightened around her mug. She threw her sister a glare which only made Serafina's smile widened.

"And why would I care about that?" Liliana snapped at her.

"Don't deny it. You like him. I don't know why you pretend otherwise. I saw how you ogled him at Alessia's wedding. You were practically drooling," Serafina said.

"Fina!" Alessia admonished their younger sister.

Liliana was too angry to respond. How dare Serafina accuse of her such a thing. *Drooling over a man. Never.*

She had made that mistake of thinking she was in love before. *Never again.*

Thankfully, the mug in her hand was ceramic and not so easily crushed in her firm grip.

"She shouldn't say such things, Mama," Alessia said to their mother.

Serafina huffed, her mouth opening to no doubt offer more choice words. She was cut off by Mama's outstretched hand.

Mama turned to Alessia. "Serafina is entitled to speak freely among us. Same as any of you. We are family."

Alessia shook her head but didn't argue. There was no arguing with Mama who, despite her protests on the matter, always seemed to indulge her youngest daughters.

Liliana turned to Serafina. "And what about Angelo?"

Serafina gave her a murderous glare. "What about him?"

"You watched him all night at the wedding."

"I did not!"

"And when he was dancing with Valentina, your whole face reddened. It looked like you were going to explode. You—"

"Liliana," Alessia cut her off with a frown.

Knowing poking their little sister further would only anger her more, Liliana sat back in her chair and sniffed. "Whatever silly notion you have of Signor Lazzaro and me, let me make my feelings clear. Signor Lazzaro is an arrogant, cocky, pompous, overdressed fool with mediocre magic skill. He thinks himself so clever. So charming. Just because he has all the strumpets in Zamerra falling over themselves."

"Liliana!" Pamina and Alessia exclaimed in unison.

Liliana lifted her chin. "I told him as much last time I saw him too."

Alessia's eyes widened in horror. "No, you did not. He's Massimo's best friend!"

"So? That doesn't give him the right to treat me like one of his..." she glanced at Fiorella, "*admirers*."

Alessia rubbed her forehead and shook her head.

"I think he's the handsomest man I've ever seen," Fiorella said in a quiet voice, a gleam in her green eyes.

Everyone turned to look at the youngest Silveri sister in surprise. Fiorella blushed under their stares.

She gave Alessia an apologetic look. "Massimo is handsome, too."

At this, the others laughed. Franny joined in, shaking so bad she spilled caffé from her tiny mug.

Pamina grabbed a cloth from the cupboard and cleaned the little spot before filling the elf's cup again.

"Now, enough teasing. Let's discuss the costumes. We should start on them right away," Mama said, leaning back in her chair.

Serafina and Fiorella squealed with delight.

Liliana fought the urge to roll her eyes. Their mother was eyeing her with interest now. No doubt, trying to read her to see if there was any truth in Serafina's words. Liliana felt her hackles rise. The image of Dante dancing at Alessia's wedding flashed in Liliana's mind. His presence had sent all the towns-folk in a tizzy. They were the ones drooling and pawing him. Giordana worst of all. They didn't seem to mind *his* magic. A double standard if there ever was one.

Her face burned at the memory of his nearness, the deep timber of his voice, and the suggestive words he'd spoken.

The shocked look on his face when she'd refused his advances had been delicious. His dark brown eyes going wide and his pouty lips parting ever so slightly.

"Liliana?" Alessia's gentle voice pulled her from her memories.

She blinked. Everyone was looking at her now.

"Did you hear what I said?" Alessia asked.

"No. What?"

A look of concern flashed on her sister's face. "Well, I just thought you should hear this from me first. Before the news starts spreading."

"What news?"

"There's a new apothecary opening up in town."

Liliana frowned. "Yes. I know. Pamina told me. What of it?"

Alessia's gaze darted away. "Well, it belongs to Dante. He bought the shop and is planning to move in within the next few weeks, I imagine."

"Oh, he's moving to Zamerra! I thought you meant he would have someone working here for him," Serafina exclaimed, sharing an excited look with Fiorella.

Liliana didn't hear what else they said. A strange buzzing sound filled her ears and her stomach flip-flopped. She felt as if the universe had pulled the rug out right from under her feet and the fates were laughing at her as she fought for balance.

Dante in Zamerra? Why? What could he possibly find in Zamerra that he couldn't in his city? And opening an apothecary? He would come with his magic and charm to upstage her. She had no doubt the townsfolk would gladly give him their business over her.

Aware of their mother's calculating gaze and her older sister's worried look, she finished off her caffé and sighed deeply, letting Pamina's magic settle her emotions.

"Oh. How nice for him," she finally said with a forced smile.

Serafina snorted. Pamina and Alessia exchanged wary glances while Fiorella frowned. Their mother didn't look fooled, but it was the best Liliana could manage.

She sat there by the fire, the heat making her clammy now. Her heart felt as if it would fly out of her chest and her instincts were screaming for her to smash something. Anything.

Dante Lazzaro opening his shop in Zamerra — her town — was a direct move to rile her. To pay her back for refusing him. She seethed. Even Pamina's magical caffé couldn't calm her down. Liliana took another deep breath and stared into the dancing flames. If it was a game he wanted, he'd learn quickly that he'd chosen the wrong witch to play with.

* * *

"I'm tired. Can we go home now?" Fiorella whined, blowing a puff of breath into the cold air.

Liliana continued plucking the giant brown mushrooms from the dirt, her back to her sister. "You volunteered to help me. We'll go back when the basket is full."

Fiorella sighed. "What do you need all these for anyway?"

"Brewing. Now, bring the basket over here please."

Her sister obeyed with a heavy sigh, dragging the near-full basket to Liliana. The earthy and rotting aroma of the fungi filled the autumn air.

"My hands are getting cold," Fiorella said as she uprooted a group of mushrooms with a flick of her wrist.

They landed atop the others with a heavy 'plop,' filling the basket. Another mushroom sprang from the dirt and shot toward them. It dropped in Liliana's lap. Then came another and another.

"Ella, stop!" Liliana exclaimed as more followed.

She jumped to her feet and covered her face as the mushrooms flew out of the ground and pelted her.

"I'm trying!" Fiorella replied, waving her arms wildly.

The air grew pungent now as the ground spit mushrooms out in rapid succession. Liliana swatted them away best as she could as she made her way to her sister.

She grabbed Fiorella's hand and gave it a squeeze. "Breathe. Focus."

"I'm trying," Fiorella said with a frustrated growl.

Seeing that her sister was growing more flustered as the mushrooms continued their mass exodus, Liliana inhaled and chanted a quick calming spell over her. Pain struck between her eyes as the magic surged through her.

Casting direct spells on people was hard and depleting, which was why she only did it for emergencies.

Fiorella stiffened as the spell hit her. Immediately, the mushrooms halted. The ones in mid-air dropped instantly in unison. The forest floor was covered with them now.

"Well, that's one way to pick mushrooms," Liliana said with a snort.

Her sister's shoulders drooped as she stared at the strewn fungi. They'd hit the ground hard, some of them broken into pieces, their dirty roots sprawling and stretching toward the sky. It looked like a massacre. A mushroom massacre.

"Come on, Ella. Let's go home," Liliana's voice softened as she placed a hand on her sister's shoulder.

Fiorella turned to her with watery eyes. "What about the..." she gestured to the broken caps and stems.

"We can't carry them all back, Ella. Maybe the deer and rabbits will have themselves a feast."

The young girl sniffled. "Or I could try and replant them. I—"

"No!" Liliana's words came out harsher than she'd meant.

Fiorella flinched and blinked rapidly, her lower lip trembling. She turned away from Liliana and picked up the overflowing basket.

"Next time, only try one at a time," Liliana said, trying to soften her voice.

Her sister faced her and nodded, doing her best to hold back her tears. Liliana searched for something encouraging to say but came up short.

Alessia and Pamina were better at comforting Fiorella. Even Serafina knew what to say in such situations.

"I'm ready to go home," Fiorella broke the silence.

Not waiting for a response, she lifted the heavy-laden

basket higher and started toward their villa. Liliana followed, sighing to herself.

She glanced over her shoulder at the mushrooms, making a note to return with another basket to collect them. It would be a shame to waste them.

Pain throbbed behind her temple as she walked. She'd need to drink one of her tonics first to ward off the effects of the spell she'd cast. Her eyes fell on Fiorella.

The young witch's power was growing stronger. With Hallow's Eve quickly approaching, there was no telling what Fiorella's magic would do. Despite her mother's assurance, Liliana had a bad feeling nothing good would come from this masquerade.

Chapter 4

A Warm Warning

Dante

Autumn had come to Zamerra, and the forested mountains had gone from luscious green to a blanket of deep red, brown, and yellow.

It had taken nearly a week to travel from coach to coach and, finally, a horse-pulled wagon cart to arrive in the mountain town. The journey had been long and tiresome, but the view was spectacular. Rivers and untouched nature surrounded the area.

All the same, Dante breathed a sigh of relief as he spotted the sprawling stone villa of his longtime friend, Massimo Gallo, the newly appointed count of Zamerra and the surrounding region.

The brown clay tiled roof matched the treetops that surrounded it, and the smoothed yellow stone was stark against the blue sky.

Dante glanced at the forking dirt road. A little further in that direction and he would be at the Silveri's villa. Would Liliana be home? Would she accept his apology in person? He'd never received a letter in return for his written attempt to make amends.

Brushing the thought aside with a grunt, he jumped down from the wagon cart. Leaves crunched under his boots as he walked up to the towering gates. The cold mountain air filled his lungs.

"Hello?" he called, peering through the iron bars of the gate.

An older man walked slowly toward him, a groundskeeper by the looks of his dirty, heavy coat and boots. He cast a wary look at Dante.

"Good afternoon, Signore. Is Count Gallo home? I've come for an impromptu visit."

The man only blinked back at him before turning away.

"Aren't you going to let me in? I'm a friend of the count. Dante Lazzaro. Hello? Signore!"

Dante's words echoed in the silence. Cold air nipped at his cheeks and nose, but the fuzzy red scarf he'd enchanted kept his neck nice and cozy. He turned to look at the brown mare he'd borrowed from the Blossom Inn's stable.

"Well, what do we now?" He asked the horse with a scoff.

It wasn't as if he could understand the mare. He would need Liliana's younger sister, Serafina, for that. The thought of her brought the image of Liliana to his mind. Her tall, slender body encased in that blood red dress. He'd always loved that color.

"Dante!" Massimo's voice rang out, interrupting his thoughts.

Dante turned to find his friend approaching the gate. Massimo opened it for him as the groundskeeper watched in the background. The fae embraced him with a hearty pat on the back and motioned him in.

"Signor Vonte, can you please see to the horse and cart?" Massimo asked the older man.

The man nodded and walked past them to lead the mare in. "Yes, Count Gallo."

Dante matched Massimo's long stride as he led him toward the large villa. Once inside and out of earshot, he turned to Massimo and nodded back toward the door they'd come through. "Suspicious fellow, isn't he?"

Massimo's amber eyes met his. "Signor Vonte? Well, you'll have to forgive him. There's still a distrust of magic in the town. I'm sure he'll come around. Many others have."

"They've accepted you as count, so that is promising. And your Contessa is a witch, after all," Dante said with a smile.

"Yes, well, as you know, despite my fae inheritance, I don't have magic of my own and neither does Alessia so that... has helped."

A grunt escaped Dante. "Yes, I imagine so. Most people are still wary of magic and those who practice it. Though they do love the products made by magic."

Massimo led him further into the villa. Dante looked around at his friend's spacious entrance and gave a low whistle. "My, isn't this an upgrade from your previous home."

Massimo rubbed his neck awkwardly, a habit he had whenever his wealth or status was mentioned. "Yes, well. We plan to fill it," he followed Dante's gaze along the painted portraits on the walls and dark wood furniture, "with children," he added quickly as if he'd given Dante the wrong impression.

The warlock's head snapped to him. "Children? Already? You've only been wed a few months. Does that mean..."

Massimo frowned. "No. We're not expecting just yet, but someday."

They fell quiet. Dante knew he should congratulate his

friend or at least offer an obligatory handshake, but the strangest feeling hit him, leaving him off-kilter.

He'd never been envious of his wealthy friend. At least not for more than a fleeting moment. But seeing Massimo standing in his beautiful villa, married and blissfully awaiting fatherhood, Dante couldn't help but imagine himself in his place.

Him? A father? He shook the silly notion from his mind.

You're a disappointment. His father's words rose to the surface.

"Are you well?" Massimo asked with a concerned look.

Before Dante could answer, a familiar meow sounded from behind them. He turned to see Massimo's gray cat, Lucia, saunter down the stairs toward them.

"Lucia!" He smiled, kneeling and holding out a hand to pet her.

She gave him an unimpressed blink and walked right past his outstretched hand. Jumping up on a cat-sized sofa, she laid herself down and turned to stare at them with a look that seemed to say 'what?.'

"Well, I see she's acclimated well to her role as a count's cat," Dante murmured, rising to his feet.

Massimo's golden cheeks reddened along with the tips of his pointed ears. "Forgive her. It's her nap time."

Dante snorted. "Ahh. I see you're already getting practice for fatherhood."

He looked around the cozy sitting room and nodded in approval. "It has a certain mountainy yet elegant charm."

"Yes, thank you. It's all Alessia's doing. Well, and Franny's of course. Our house elf."

Massimo pointed to the carved white stone fireplace where a fire blazed. "I did help choose the design for that."

"And it suits the room perfectly. I like the swirls and loops.

Say, where is your lovely Contessa?" Dante asked, glancing around.

"She's visiting with her Mama and sisters. Organizing the upcoming masquerade. There's much to be done. Do you believe your shop will be opened before then?"

Growing warm near the fire, Dante took off his scarf and set it down on one of the coffee tables.

"I'm hoping to be moved in there by the end of the week."

"Do you need help? With the moving or unpacking?" Massimo asked, motioning Dante to one of the upholstered armchairs.

Dante sank into the soft cushion. "Are you offering your personal services? Don't you have people to do that for you now? You are the count, after all."

Massimo gave him a flat look. "I'm perfectly capable of carrying some boxes, Dante."

The warlock chuckled. "I appreciate the offer, but I had everything sent to the shop aside from my traveling bags. As for the unpacking, I prefer to do it myself so I can organize it to my liking."

"Right. Well, I should warn you, not everyone in Zamerra is... excited about your apothecary opening. It might take some time for certain people to come around."

"Certain people? Such as?" Dante asked, unable to hide the amusement in his voice.

"Well, there's the pharmacist. Signor Marcello. He's less than pleased about more competition."

"More? Who is he competing with now?"

Massimo met his stare. "I think you know very well who. I don't know what you said to Liliana, but I did warn you that she wasn't one to trifle with, Dante."

A sigh escaped Dante. "Yes, so I've learned. I may have made a suggestive comment or two," he waved his hands in an appeasing gesture at Massimo's darkening look. "It was the strawberry wine talking. Anyways, I did write an apology and I've already rehearsed my sincerest lines for when I see her again."

Massimo frowned. "It's not a game, Dante. She's Alessia's sister. My sister now, as well. You put me in a difficult position. Please, leave her alone. There are plenty of other women in Zamerra to pursue. Though again, I warn you, I can't let you make a... nuisance of yourself."

Dante met his friend's stern look and scoffed. "Massimo, I'm insulted. You make it sound like I'm an unwanted pest."

"Of course not. You're my dearest friend, but you do have a reputation..."

At this Dante rolled his eyes and waved off the fae's words. "Why does everyone keep saying that? I'm a changed man. I swear."

Massimo nodded approvingly. "Good. Now, that that's settled, would you like some caffé?"

The warlock smiled. "I was wondering when you'd remember your manners."

Ignoring his quip, Massimo led him into the hall and into the large kitchen.

Sunlight streamed in from the giant arched windows above the wide sink and dark wooden counters. A fire blazed from the white hearth carved out of the stone wall. It filled the room with its cozy warmth. Gloves of garlic and dried herbs hung from hooks in the wooden beams of the ceiling along with various baskets and pots.

A little house elf stood atop the long wooden table in the center of the room, rolling pasta dough. She looked up at their entrance, her beady brown eyes darting between the two from beneath her pointed red hat.

"Hello, Franny. This is my friend, Dante. Signor Lazzaro.

We were just about to have caffé. Would you like some?" Massimo asked the little elf as he opened a cupboard.

Franny replied in elvish and pointed to the silver carafe sitting in the corner of the kitchen on its own counter. She pushed her brown braid over her shoulder and wiped her little hands on her white apron.

Massimo handed Dante a ceramic mug and kept one for himself.

"My. Mountain life has changed you. Where are your servants?" Dante asked as he followed Massimo over to the counter to pour himself a cup.

His friend shrugged. "I couldn't very well ask them to make the move with me. They have families and lives in the city. Besides, Alessia and I can manage everything ourselves and we have Franny."

They looked at the elf who had been watching them. She glanced away quickly, giggling to herself as she got back to work.

Dante took a sip from his mug and savored the sweet, smooth liquid.

A murmur of approval escaped him. An instant jolt of alertness filled him, heightening his senses.

Massimo gave him a knowing look. "Pamina's special brew."

At the mention of Liliana's sister, a vision of Liliana herself flashed in Dante's mind. Her dark brown, alluring eyes and mass of black curls that framed her angular face.

"Dante? Do you want more sugar?" Massimo's words interrupted his wandering thoughts.

He blinked at the spoon his friend held up to him and nodded in reply. The sugar swirled in his cup, spoon stirring on its own.

"Ah. Enchanted silverware. That does make things easier.

And how do your subjects feel about such things?" Dante asked before taking the spoon out and handing it back to Massimo.

"Well, they're just as hesitant about magic as some of the city folk are. We hope to change that with this masquerade. Show them that magic, used responsibly and in moderation, isn't something to fear."

"Hmm."

Massimo's amber eyes searched him. "What?"

Dante shrugged. "I didn't say anything."

"Yes and that's suspicious. You always have something to say."

Taking a seat at the end of the long table, Dante set his mug down, careful not to disturb Franny's work. Massimo joined him.

"You think it's a bad idea?" He pressed Dante.

"I think... you have the right heart. I only worry that gathering everyone together on Hallow's Eve could have the opposite effect of what you're trying to do. Magic will be at its peak, even harder to harness and control than it usually is. At the very least, you should have safeguards in place."

"I see. Well, then I'm grateful you've arrived just in time to help me."

"Did I miss the part where I volunteered my assistance?" Dante teased.

Massimo shrugged off his words. "Well, obviously, I'll pay you for your work. Anything you need. The last thing I want is to put Alessia or anyone else in Zamerra at risk."

"I'll need to gather some more supplies, but I think I should be able to have everything ready before then."

His friend nodded. "Excellent. Anything you can't find in town or the surrounding area, I can order."

Dante glanced at the window. "Let me check my inventory

and the local ingredients and then I'll let you know what else we'll need."

"Very good. I'd invite you to stay over for supper, but we've made plans already. Another night though if you're available."

"Dinner with the family?" Dante asked, drumming his fingers on the table.

Massimo gave him a wary look. "Yes, but as I told you before, I think it would be wise to keep your distance from Liliana. At least until she's warmed up to the idea of you living here."

"Yes. Yes. I understand. I swear I'll be on my best behavior," Dante promised.

Chapter 5

A Chance Encounter
Liliana

C ool autumn air filled Liliana's lungs as she walked through the forest behind their villa. This time, she came alone. The oak trees towered above her, their canopies of red, brown, and orange blocking the darkening sky. Dead leaves and undergrowth crunched beneath her boots as she went, and the smell of damp and dirt enveloped her.

Though she didn't have plant or earth magic, she could feel a strange stirring in the air. The forest held many secrets. Fiorella would know them better than her. The voice of the woods that used to speak to her youngest sister never spoke to her.

Twigs snapped behind Liliana, making her pause. The unmistakable sound of heavy footsteps startled her, drawing nearer. It couldn't be any of her sisters. Perhaps it was Massimo going for his daily walk. Though he always went early in the morning and headed for town, not the woods.

Liliana turned, hand at her side and ready to cast a spell.

A bird squawked overhead, catching her eye. Then silence.

The footsteps paused and a soft curse, undeniably male and not Massimo, followed.

"Who's there?" Liliana demanded.

"Hello?" the voice returned, the sound echoing through the trees.

It was a deep, rich voice. A familiar voice.

The man or rather, warlock, attached to it appeared before her. *Dante Lazzaro.* He looked just as startled to see her but recovered quickly with a wide smile and a tip of his hat in greeting.

Liliana scowled. "What are you doing here? Are you following me?" She couldn't hide the irritation in her voice.

Dante, still smiling, strutted toward her with all the confidence and show of a peacock. Liliana snorted at the thought. An accurate description given his inclination to wearing hats with ridiculously long feathers.

"I didn't know I'd find you here, Signorina. Honestly," Dante replied, spreading his arms in an appeasing gesture.

"What are you doing here?" Liliana asked again, meeting his gaze.

His smile faltered. "I came to see what kind of local ingredients are here. For my shop."

Liliana felt her lip curl. "There are woods closer to town."

Dante sighed. "Yes, but the magic is stronger in these woods. I didn't mean to disturb you. Perhaps you would be kind enough to show me your—"

"The only thing I will *show* you, Signor Lazzaro, is the path back to town," Liliana said with a huff.

The warlock's dark eyebrow arched. "I was going to say your fungi supply. What were you implying?"

Heat rose up Liliana's neck. The amused smirk on Dante's face only added fuel to her anger. He thought himself so clever. *So irresistible.*

"Well, given our last conversation, you can't blame me for thinking so poorly of you," she shot back.

Regret flashed across his features. "I suppose not. Did you receive my letter?"

"Yes."

"You didn't send a reply."

"No. I didn't."

Dante's lips pursed into a frown. "I shouldn't have been so forward with you. In my defense, I had one too many drinks and I had the impression you were feeling it as well. The attraction, I mean. Not the wine. Do you accept my sincerest apology?"

"If I say yes, will you leave now?" Liliana asked, holding her head high.

He snorted. "I have just as much right to walk this forest as you do. There are plenty of ingredients for us both. Besides, I'm on a mission. Massimo asked for my help in preparing for Hallow's Eve."

"What do you mean help?"

Dante shrugged and glanced around the darkening woods. "You know. The usual. Talismans. Barriers. Don't want any of the townsfolk to get possessed or die of fright when they see their first spirit. I'm sure..."

Liliana didn't listen as he prattled on. Why hadn't Alessia and Massimo asked for her help? Did they think Dante's magic was stronger than hers? He'd been there only a few days and already he was trying to usurp her place.

"How gracious of you," she interrupted him, her hand going to her hip.

Dante paused, dark eyes studying her warily. "Er... yes?"

"Moving to our little town to help us poor, uneducated mountain folk. I don't know how we've managed this long without you and your talismans. Is that what you spent all those years at the academia of warlocks learning?"

"It was the Academia of the Magical Arts, actually, and you're mocking me."

Liliana shrugged. "I don't like you."

The warlock snorted. "Yes. You've made that quite clear. You think I'm a... *pompous peacock,* was that right?"

"I don't recall."

Silence stretched between them. Seeing that he wasn't going anywhere, Liliana turned her back to him and continued deeper into the forest. He followed.

Not only did he have the nerve to tag along but he started whistling. The sharp, merry tune grated on her nerves. She had no doubt he was trying to get under her skin. It was working, too.

Liliana threw him a dark look. "If you must stalk me, can't you do it in silence?"

Dante frowned. "Don't tell me you don't like music."

"That is not music."

The warlock caught up to her, matching her long stride. He glanced over at her and grinned. "What kind of music do you prefer? And if you've already told me, I apologize. My memory gets fuzzy after a few glasses of wine."

She looked away and kept walking, growing irritated by his smoky, cedar-like scent that permeated the air around him. There was no denying he was handsome. Tall. Rich brown skin. Dark curls that framed his flawless face and eyes that shone with perpetual mirth. His lips were full and unfairly hypnotic as they moved, which they did often. Too often. Liliana hated him for all of it and she hated herself for noticing these things.

"I prefer the ballads myself. Especially the love ballads," he continued on, oblivious of her inner turmoil.

"Of course, you do."

He looked at her in earnest, his brown eyes drilling into her. "Don't you believe in love? I thought everyone did."

A harsh laugh escaped her. "Love is for fairytales."

He smiled. "Normally, I'd agree, but I have to admit, seeing Massimo with your sister," he shook his head and stared straight ahead, "makes me wonder if I'm wrong. Maybe it's true... for some people."

Caught off guard by his openness, Liliana nearly missed the circle of mushrooms in the forest clearing. She stopped suddenly and knelt down to inspect them.

"A Fairy ring? You could have told me that's what we were looking for," Dante said, squatting beside her.

Liliana glanced at him. "*We* aren't looking for anything. I don't need your assistance. Please feel free to leave any moment."

"My, you are a difficult woman. I almost expect you to start hissing at me."

"Would you leave me alone if I did?"

An irritated sigh escaped Dante. "Is my presence really that bothersome to you?"

Instead of answering, Liliana turned her attention back to the red-top mushrooms. All of them were the same size, nearly identical.

"How many portals to Fairy are in the forest?" Dante asked, suddenly growing serious.

Liliana met his gaze. "Just this one."

"Well, that's a relief. I'd offer my assistance to close it, but you've made it quite clear that you don't need my help."

Ignoring his comment, Liliana closed her eyes and spread her hands above the small circle. She chanted a spell, drawing on her magic. A hot surge of power ripped through her as she cast it.

Closing the portal to Fairy entirely would take at least

another day and another spell, but she had time. The magic of the mushrooms was dormant on their side, but with Hallow's Eve approaching, Liliana didn't want to risk something coming through.

The fae in Fairy were wild and dangerous. Nothing like her gentle half-fae brother-in-law Massimo.

"Very impressive," Dante's deep voice snapped her back to the present.

She opened her eyes to find him staring at her, his eyes smoldering with undeniable desire. A shiver of awareness ran up her spine. They were alone in the forest with night approaching and the words he'd spoken to her at her sister's wedding rang in her ears, making her face warm.

He'd told her he wanted to taste her. To touch her. Then he'd gone and danced with Giordana Bellefonte, as if his words had meant nothing. They were as empty as his head and the letter he'd sent was short and rehearsed. He didn't even remember what he'd told her. How many other women had received the same apology?

Pushing away the memories, Liliana rose to her feet and brushed the dirt off her dress. She glanced around at the darkening forest, pulling her shawl tighter as the cold air swirled around them.

"I could use your help," Dante's words surprised her.

Her brow furrowed. "My help? With what?"

He gestured to the mushroom circle behind her. "Setting up barriers. Safeguards. Before the masquerade."

"What makes you think I'd help you?"

Dante sighed heavily. "Come on, I thought we were making progress here. You can't hate me forever. Like I said, it was the wine talking. It was a lot of wine. I could have been sweet talking a cow and not known it."

Liliana's jaw clenched. "And this is supposed to improve my opinion of you?"

He rubbed his forehead and groaned. "What must I do to regain your favor? Do you want me to get down on one knee and beg?"

Liliana huffed. "I don't want anything from you. You're the one who keeps following me."

He shot her a glare. "I wasn't following you. At first, anyway. I'm not some creep who preys on women."

"Aren't you?"

Dante's face hardened. "Most women find me charming."

Liliana snorted.

Ignoring her, he continued, "Whether you like me or not, it would benefit everyone if we worked together on this. I can pay you for your time, of course, and before you tell me off, again, you should know I have a cauldron."

"I have my own cauldron."

"Mine is better."

Liliana balled her fist, fighting the urge to smash it into his stupid, handsome face. Why did he enjoy vexing her so?

His gaze darted to her clenched hand and back to her face. "No offense. I only mean that my cauldron is made of enchanted silver."

That was indeed impressive, but Liliana wasn't about to let him know it. Silver enhanced spells in a way her iron cauldron couldn't.

Schooling her features, she sniffed and lifted her chin. "I do just fine with my cauldron. There's something to be said about one's magic skill if you have to use such... enhancements."

Anger flashed on the warlock's face, making Liliana smirk. She was beginning to see why he enjoyed riling her.

"There's nothing wrong with my magic skills, I can assure you." His voice deepened as he took a step toward her.

He stood so close now. His scent enveloped her, making her lightheaded. Woodsy. Strong. A curl hung low from his tall hat, bouncing in front of his narrowed, dark eyes. His lips were pursed and dangerously close. One more step and a tilt of her head and they'd be on hers.

Heat spread through her. She needed to go, but her legs wouldn't move. Despite the cold air, she was burning up.

"Fine," she heard herself answer, shocking them both.

"Fine? Does that mean you're agreeing to help me?" Dante asked, staring at her in bewilderment.

"I can't leave it all up to you, can I? This is my home after all," she added, gruffly.

His face broke into a smile, making her heart skip. Liliana scowled, cursing her body for reacting to him.

"When should I expect you in the shop?" He asked, taking the lead back toward the villas.

Liliana gave him a side glance as she caught up to him. "What would I need to come to your *apothecary* for? I can make my own tonics and spells."

Dante sighed. "If we're going to work together, I think we should work closely."

"As professionals, of course. You have my word, I'll be a perfect gentleman," he added at her dark glare.

Liliana bit back the harsh words on her tongue. *His word.* She would be a fool to believe anything he told her, but he was right about one thing. Working with him would benefit Zamerra, and she'd do anything to keep her family safe. Even if it meant suffering *him.*

Chapter 6

Preparations

Dante

"Are you sure this is a good idea?" Massimo asked for what seemed like the hundredth time.

Dante set a glass vial carefully on the shelf and turned to look at the worried fae. "It was her idea."

His friend gave him a skeptical look.

"Well, maybe it was mine, but she agreed to it. There's nothing to be concerned about. It's just business."

"Hmm. Aren't you the one who told me you should never mix business with pleasure?"

Dante grinned. "No. It was '*always make pleasure your business*'."

Massimo opened his mouth to object, but Dante cut him off with an impatient wave.

"Not in this case. I know. I know. I can be professional, you know. This will be strictly business," he added, reaching for another vial to set out.

Massimo nodded and helped unload the last crate of tonics. "Maybe this is a good thing. If you've mended things with her that will make things much easier. Especially family dinners."

Dante turned to him. "Am I invited to family dinner now?"

"Well, as long as you and Liliana are getting along, I don't see why not."

A smile spread on Dante's face. Dinner with them sounded much more enjoyable than eating alone in the little back kitchen where he brewed his potions.

Stepping back to admire his work, he took a deep breath. The deep blue and reddish-brown glass of the vials gave the little shop a pop of color it desperately needed. Sunlight poured in from the wide storefront windows, casting a golden glow on the dark wood shelves and cabinets behind the long, freshly painted black paneled counter.

The white marble slab he'd installed on top of the black counter had cost him a fortune, but looking at the finished product now, Dante knew he'd made the right choice. He couldn't wait for Liliana to see it.

"It looks wonderful," Massimo said, echoing his thoughts.

The wall-to-wall shelves on the opposite side of the room held glass jars and baskets of raw ingredients, filling the room with the clashing smell of spices, herbs, and honey. A full-length mirror stood in the corner near the samples of beauty products.

"Is this everything then?" Massimo's question echoed in the little store.

Dante turned to him. "For now. I don't think Zamerra is quite ready for some of my products. I won't put out the enchanted objects yet. I think I'll save those for after Hallow's Eve."

"Good idea. Speaking of Hallow's Eve, have you made a list of supplies you'll need to prepare the talismans and everything else?"

"There's no need. We have everything we need here.

Speaking of preparations, did you know there was a Fairy gate in the woods behind your villa?"

Massimo's amber eyes met his. "Yes, but as far as I can tell it's dormant. Why?"

"Are there any other portals nearby? The river? The mountains?"

"I... I'm not sure. Should I go and investigate?"

Dante shook his head. "With your fae blood, you would have already found them, I'm sure. But, just to be safe, I'll ask Liliana to help me perform a spell. Make sure there are no hidden portals or surprises."

Massimo frowned. "I thought the spirits didn't need portals to cross over on Hallow's Eve."

"The benevolent ones don't. They're granted their freedom to come and go as they please on that night, but the wickedest ones sometimes escape through the portals. I suppose the Lady of Death's guards need a break too."

His friend shuddered. "Death. Wicked spirits on the loose. I'm beginning to wonder if this masquerade is such a good idea after all."

"Don't worry. We'll have Zamerra well secured. I—"

Dante was cut off by the bell announcing someone's arrival. He looked up to see a group of women enter, their whispers loud in the silence. None of their faces looked familiar to him. Pushing back his disappointment, Dante offered them a warm smile and nod.

"Welcome! I haven't officially opened my shop yet, but please feel free to look around and I'm here if you have any questions."

One of the women stepped away from the others and approached him with a wide smile.

She curtsied to Massimo. "Count Gallo."

"Good day, Signora Bellefonte." The fae smiled politely in return and nodded to the other women watching.

Turning her attention to Dante, her eyes lit up. "Signor Lazzaro! It's so good to see you again. And on a permanent basis. I hope you've been well?"

"Yes. Thank you. It's good to see you as well, Signorina." Dante returned her smile, trying to remember when he'd last seen her. The last time he'd been in Zamerra was for Massimo and Alessia's wedding and the only woman's face he could recall with any real clarity was Liliana's.

Her long-lashed, brown eyes flashed in his mind. The memory of her upturned face and dark curls spilling loose around her as she chanted in the woods made his pulse quicken.

"Signor Lazzaro?" the woman's voice interrupted his thoughts.

Dante glanced at Massimo for help.

"Signor Lazzaro wouldn't miss a masquerade. He'll be there," his friend answered for him.

"Well then, I look forward to sharing another dance, Signore," Signorina Bellefonte said with a pretty smile.

The other young women giggled behind her. Massimo shot him a warning look. Her words brought back the vague memory of their dance though try as he could, Dante couldn't remember much. All he saw was Liliana. She'd only danced once the entire night, but it had been the most hypnotic dance he'd ever witnessed.

"Signor Lazzaro!" a cheerful young voice called as the bell rang.

Everyone turned to see the newcomers. It was Liliana's family. Signora entered along with Liliana's sisters- Alessia, Pamina, Serafina, and Fiorella. All of them except for Liliana.

"Well, isn't this a pleasant surprise! But hold on, aren't you missing someone?" Dante asked, pasting on a smile to mask his disappointment.

Alessia and Pamina exchanged a look.

Signora Silveri smiled warmly at him. "Liliana was too busy with her talismans. She sends her best regards, Signor."

"Sure, she does," the auburn-haired Serafina said with a snort. She stared back at the other women in the shop, who were eyeing the sisters warily.

Irritation filled Dante at the news. *Stubborn woman.* Was she really that determined to stay away from him?

He watched as Alessia greeted Massimo with a kiss on the cheek and the other girls spread out to inspect his shop.

"Oh! It's so beautiful," the youngest one, Fiorella, said, her green eyes widening as she took it all in.

Serafina nodded. "Much better than before." She turned to Dante. "You have good taste, Signor."

Signorina Bellefonte frowned at the girl's frankness, exchanging a look with her friends. Disapproving murmurs followed.

Ignoring them, Dante smiled at the young Silveri girl. "Thank you. I've always thought so."

Alessia, who'd walked over to stand protectively beside her sisters, gave him a kind smile. "We appreciate your help with the masquerade, Signor."

He waved away her words. "Please, it's my pleasure, Contessa."

Reminded of Alessia's status, the other women's whispers stopped.

Dante turned to them. "Forgive me, signore, but I'm afraid I'll have to ask you to leave now. The shop isn't quite ready yet. Come back tomorrow and I'll be happy to assist you."

He gave them a dazzling smile, hoping to soften the dismissal.

Signorina Bellefonte smiled back, eyes traveling up and down his body.

Normally, Dante appreciated the attention and would happily flirt in return, but he was keenly aware of Liliana's mother and sisters watching their exchange. The thought of them reporting everything back to her prompted him to hold his tongue.

If he could convince Liliana he could be professional maybe she wouldn't be so insistent about working on her own.

The women curtsied to Massimo and Alessia and nodded farewell to Dante as they took their leave. The bell jingled as they left, the cold air swirling in briefly.

"You're not interested in Signorina Bellefonte, are you?" Serafina's question caught him off guard.

Alessia sucked in a breath. "Fina!"

All eyes turned to Dante. He felt his mouth twitch in amusement at the young girl's boldness.

He faced her. "Not particularly, why do you ask?"

"Because she's a stuck-up, vain twit. You can do much better than her."

"Serafina, that's a horrible thing to say," Pamina spoke up, frowning at her younger sister.

The girl shrugged. "Well, it's true."

Alessia turned to Dante, face reddening. "Forgive her, Signore. She forgets her manners." She shot Serafina a glare.

"Well, I think a woman who speaks her mind is very admirable and please. Also, call me Dante. We're all friends here."

He smiled at them. The Silveris were a refreshing and entertaining bunch, but he couldn't help but feel the loss of Liliana's presence. What could he do to get on the witch's good side? Her narrowed eyes flashed in his mind. Her pursed lips. Lips that looked so soft despite the sharp words they spewed.

"What kind of tonics do you make? Can you do spells?" Serafina asked, interrupting his wandering thoughts.

"I make all kinds of tonics and salves. Mostly healing, sometimes beauty products. As far as spells—"

"Beauty products? Do you have something that can take away my freckles?" Serafina cut him off, her eyed darting around the shop.

Dante met Signora Silveri's gaze for permission. She frowned at the young witch.

Serafina, catching her mother's look, huffed. "I'm almost sixteen. I'm not a child anymore. Why can't I use magic to cover my face if I want to?"

Her mother's eyebrows knitted together. "You don't need magic to cover your face, *amore.*"

Serafina opened her mouth to argue but was cut short by her Mama's warning look.

Bottom lip curling in anger, she stomped over to inspect the herbs and spices on the shelves. Fiorella joined her.

Signora Silveri turned to Dante, her gaze sharp and calculating. "I don't believe magic should be used or relied on for everyday things. You never know what could happen."

Dante frowned. "While I understand your hesitance, Signora, I assure you, there's nothing dangerous with my products. They're harmless."

Massimo, who'd been silently watching, cleared his throat. "Speaking of your products, we should let you finish setting up your shop. There's much to do before the masquerade."

Alessia smiled at her husband, sharing a loving look that made Dante's heart twist. Pamina walked over to usher the younger girls out.

"We'd love to have you over soon for dinner, Signor Lazzaro. Perhaps another evening?" Signora Silveri asked, giving Dante a friendly smile.

Dante smiled back. "I'd love that, thank you, Signora. Please, wish your daughter well for me. Tell her I look forward to seeing her in my shop. Soon, I hope."

Signora Silveri's eyes gleamed. "Of course. I'll pass on your regards."

"Good bye!" the other girls called as they headed for the door.

Massimo brought up the rear, pausing to look back at Dante with a sympathetic look. "I'll check back tomorrow to see how you're doing. Let me know if you need anything."

Dante nodded in response and watched them go. Silence filled the shop. After locking the storefront and drawing the curtains closed, Dante blinked against the darkness. With a quick chant, he lit the candles along the wall.

Sighing, he made his way to the back room to start unpacking the rest of his personal belongings. The little kitchen was colder than the front. Grayish light filtered in through the small window above the sink and the smell of ash drifted from the empty hearth on the opposite side of the room.

Walking to the little table in the center, Dante's eyes caught on a glass vial inside the wooden crate. It was Signora Gavella's love potion. It needed a label before he put it on the shelf. Making a mental note to do so before morning, he picked it up and held it up to his nose. It smelled like burnt leaves and smoke.

"So, that's what love smells like, huh?"

The words of the older witch replayed in his mind. *It will lead you to your true match.*

A snort escaped him. The thought of being bonded to someone for life made Dante cringe inward. He'd only disappoint them. Before his father's words could play out over and over, he pushed the thoughts away.

Zamerra was a new place. A new start.

Chapter 7

A Sticky Predicament
Liliana

L iliana packed the last of her supplies into the crate and took a sip from her mug. The caffé had turned cold, but the smooth, sugary taste was still very much satisfying.

"Are you going to take that to Dante's shop?" Fiorella asked, walking over to have a look.

Liliana frowned at her. "You mean Signor Lazzaro?"

Her sister shrugged. "He said we could call him by his first name."

"Of course, he did," Liliana muttered, fighting the urge to roll her eyes.

"Can I go with you? Please?" Fiorella asked, a hopeful look on her face.

Liliana's brow arched. She wanted to say no but maybe having Fiorella there as a buffer would be a good thing. At least it would deter the warlock from trying to openly flirt with her. Hopefully.

As much as she hated it, she couldn't deny the fact that her body, traitor that it was, reacted to him. His dark eyes and smiling lips filled her mind. Pushing such images away, she turned to her sister.

"Alright, but I'm leaving now. Are you ready?"

Fiorella squealed and nodded. "I'll get Serafi—"

"No. Just you and it's going to be a quick stop, Ella." Liliana cut her off.

She didn't want Serafina coming along and blabbing who-knew-what to the warlock. Picking up the wooden crate, she nodded for Fiorella to open the back door for her.

Cold air hit them as they stepped outside. The smell of far-off chimney smoke and crisp leaves filled Liliana's lungs as they headed for the stables. Fiorella helped hitch the wagon to their old horse Fabrizio.

Liliana glanced up at the gray sky, hoping there wasn't a storm coming. She wanted to get back to the forest to work on the Fairy portal. They didn't have time to waste, especially with Hallow's Eve quickly approaching. She wanted to have every-thing ready as soon as possible. The faster they got done placing the protection spells and readying talismans, the sooner she could get back to ignoring the annoying warlock.

He'd only been back in town for a week and already all the townswomen were chittering and giggling like a bunch of desperate hens.

"Wait until you see his shop! It's so beautiful," Fiorella's words snapped her back to attention.

Liliana set the crate into the back of the wagon cart and climbed up to take the reins. Fiorella followed and sat beside her on the wooden bench. She clasped her hands together in her lap and turned to Liliana with a wide smile.

"He's going to be so happy to see you."

Liliana snorted. Fabrizio threw his head back and snorted too before he started toward their gate. The gang of outdoor cats descended upon them followed by Gio, the scrappy little dog. Fabrizio stomped, scattering them away from the path.

Fiorella frowned. "He said he wanted you to come to his shop. Don't you want to see what kind of tonics and salves he can make?"

Liliana pulled Fabrizio to a stop and hopped down. "Anything he can make, so can I. Probably better than him."

She didn't hear her sister's response as she walked over to open their gate. Returning to the wagon, she saw Serafina and Pamina coming out the back door of the kitchen.

With a wave to them, she led Fabrizio outside of the gates and onto the dirt path. Fiorella jumped down to shut the gate behind them before climbing back up onto the wagon.

Fresh, cold mountain air filled their lungs as Fabrizio took off in a slow trot down the path. Fiorella hugged her wool shawl tighter around her shoulders and scooted closer to Liliana.

She looked at the fallen leaves along the path and sighed. "I don't like Autumn. So many plants die."

Liliana gave her a sideways glance. "Yes, but they come back to life in the Spring. Death is a part of life, Ella."

Her sister hugged herself, a troubled look on her young face. "I know, but I don't like it."

Not knowing how best to respond, Liliana let the conversation end there. The sound of the wagon wheels crunching the dried leaves on the path filled the silence. Smoke from the town drifted toward them along with the unmistakable smell of freshly baked bread.

"Wait until you see his shop. It's so pretty," Fiorella said with an excited smile.

"Yes. So, you've said," Liliana muttered.

The truth was, she was curious to see what the warlock was selling in his apothecary. Though it didn't seem fair to her that the townsfolk were happily welcoming him into their midst, potions and all, while she got dark looks and rude comments about her uncontrollable hair.

Knowing him, he was probably lapping all the attention right up.

Pushing such thoughts away, Liliana focused on the dirt path before them. Before long, they were past their neighbor's villa and nearing town.

Zamerra was nestled in the valley of the forested mountains with only one road in and out. The sight of the clustered stone and brick villas, tiled roofs, and cobblestoned streets made Liliana sigh. Though it was a beautiful sight, going into town always made her wary.

Not all of the townsfolk were welcoming to the *Silveri witches*.

She'd grown up an outsider because of her magic and in return had rejected the community. Her mother and sisters were too forgiving of the town's prejudices against them.

Fabrizio's hooves clomped noisily on the cobblestone as they entered town. Only a few people milled about, glancing up at their arrival. Some waved politely while others just stared.

Fiorella wriggled her gloved fingers, glancing at the dead plants and flowers in the various pots and planters.

"Don't," Liliana warned her.

The younger girl didn't meet her eyes. "I wasn't going to. I'm no fool, Liliana."

Giving her sister an approving nod, Liliana led Fabrizio down another street toward the new apothecary.

"I know you're not, Ella. I just want you to be careful," she said as she pulled their wagon to a stop.

"Good day, Signorine! Fancy meeting you in town," a cheerful voice called, catching their attention.

Their neighbors, Salvatore and Adriano Rossi, walked

toward them, arms full of brown paper sacks. Adriano's giant faun hooves stuck out of his trousers, echoing on the stone.

"Hello!" Fiorella and Liliana greeted them in return.

"We were just heading back up the mountain. Are you here to see the new apothecary?" Salvatore asked, curiosity shining in his dark eyes.

"Actually, I brought some of my own products for Signor Lazzaro's new shop. He asked for my help," Liliana explained, nodding toward the crate behind them in the cart.

The two men exchanged surprised looks.

"Ahh. How nice of you," Salvatore said, stepping closer with a mischievous smile, "you just missed Signor Marcello. He came in to have a look at his competition."

"And offer his opinion as well," Adriano added with a shake of his head.

Salvatore nodded at his husband's words and looked at Liliana. "You'll have to hear the whole story. Signor Lazzaro has agreed to dinner with us tomorrow evening, please join us. Bring your Mama and sisters. We'd love to have you."

Fiorella squealed with delight. "Oh, yes! Thank you, Signore."

Liliana, not wanting to be rude to their neighbors, gave them a hesitant smile. "Thank you for the invitation. I'll have to check with Mama first."

Dinner with Dante in attendance was the last thing she wanted to do. The less time she spent around him, the better.

Waving goodbye, the two men walked toward their own wagon.

"Well, are you ready?" Fiorella asked, jumping down to the ground.

"As ready as I'll ever be," Liliana answered with a heavy sigh.

She stepped down and tied Fabrizio to the post before

getting the crate out of the cart. Fiorella led the way to the store-front. A group of people, mostly women, crowded around the entrance. They turned to look at Liliana and her sister with mixed reactions. Some smiled and nodded politely while others scowled.

Head held high, Liliana led Fiorella past them and into the shop. A bell rang above them as they entered. More townsfolk milled about the store, filling the little space.

Dante stood behind the counter, leaning forward and engrossed in a conversation with one of the young women.

Liliana couldn't help but admire the dark wood shelves and cupboards behind him and the white marble counter he leaned on. The contrast of white on top of the black counter panels was eye-catching. There was a slight smell of fresh paint underneath the clashing aroma of herbs, vanilla scented candles, and various soaps.

As beautiful as the shop was, Liliana's gaze snagged on Dante. He looked annoyingly handsome in his white woolen sweater, with his dark curls skillfully coiling around his face.

"I don't think you need any of my skin products, Signora. Your skin is flawless. However, if you're interested in long-lasting lip color, I have some I can recommend." His deep voice carried through the shop.

"Oh, thank you, Signor Lazzaro," the woman crooned.

Liliana rolled her eyes. He was selling magical beauty products? Why was she even surprised?

Seeing that he was much too busy flirting, she motioned for Fiorella to the back room. Surely, he wouldn't mind if she set her talismans there. She wasn't going to waste her day waiting for him to acknowledge her.

Fiorella hesitated, her hand on the knob. She glanced at Dante and back to Liliana.

"It's fine. We'll just set this back there and leave. He's obviously too busy," Liliana reassured her.

Shrugging, Fiorella opened the door for Liliana and shut it quickly behind her.

Sunlight streamed in from the little kitchen window. A dying fire flickered from the hearth, filling the room with the smell of burning wood and ash. There was a hint of mint and candlewax in the air, too.

Voices drifted from the front as Liliana set her crate down on top of his round kitchen table. Fiorella picked up a vial of black liquid that stood on the tabletop and held it up to the grayish light.

"Liliana, look! It's a love potion," she said excitedly, holding out the little glass out to her sister.

She pointed to the fancy written label.

Liliana snorted. "Love potions and beauty products. I hope he actually knows how to brew something helpful. Or at least perform some defense spells."

"Do you think he meant to put it out front to sell?" Fiorella asked, taking a sniff of the corked vial.

"How should I know? Now, put that back, Ella. I want to get home."

"Shh! Listen," Fiorella said, motioning Liliana to be quiet.

Liliana frowned. "What is it? I don't hear anything."

The front shop had grown silent. Had everyone left?

Fiorella ignored her and walked over to the sink, still holding the vial in her hand. "Oh, look!"

"Ella, we have to go," Liliana whispered, glancing at the closed door.

Setting the love potion down on the counter, Fiorella reached into the sink and picked up a small potted plant. She turned to show Liliana.

"*Santos!* What is that?" Liliana said with a gasp.

It had a thick green stalk with two large leaves sprouting from each side and a bulbous red petaled head with sharp spiked edges pressed together in the middle, giving the appearance of teeth.

"I think it's a baby," Fiorella answered, green eyes lighting up on it.

The plant's head opened wide, giving them a view of the its inner green 'mouth.' Then it slammed its teeth-like spikes shut.

"Put it down, Ella. Carefully," Liliana said, eyeing it warily.

Fiorella's brow furrowed. "I didn't do this. I swear. It was alive like this before I picked it up."

"Put—"

Liliana was cut off by the door swinging open. Startled, Fiorella backed up toward the sink, bumping the vial of love potion down. Before Liliana could stop it, the glass fell and shattered on the wooden floor.

Fiorella set the plant down on the counter quickly, eyes widening in horror at the growing black puddle near her boot.

"Was that one of my potions or yours?" Dante asked casually, entering the kitchen.

Liliana bit back a groan. "I'm afraid you're going to need to make more love potion."

Dante's eyes snapped to hers.

"I'm sorry!" Fiorella said, bending down to pick up the glass.

"No! I'll get it. Who knows what is in that," Liliana told her, looking around for a rag.

Dante walked over to inspect the mess and looked at Fiorella. "No worries. I can clean it up. Are you all right?"

Fiorella nodded, eyes downcast.

Giving her sister a reassuring smile, Dante flicked his wrist over the broken glass and transferred the pieces to the waste bin. Liliana bit back the comment on her tongue. Using magic to clean up such a small mess was lazy.

The black goo didn't budge.

"Hmm. That's strange," the warlock muttered, eyes narrowing on the mess.

"Don't you have a rag or something to use? You do own cleaning supplies, don't you?" Liliana asked.

His dark eyes met hers. "Of course. In the cupboard."

Liliana opened the wooden cupboard he indicated and wet the rag in the sink. The little snapping plant seemed to be watching her though it didn't have any visible eyes.

"Here, let me," Dante said as she turned toward them with the cloth.

Their hands touched briefly, making Liliana's heart jump. She let him take it and stepped out of his way.

"It doesn't seem to be coming off," Dante said with a perplexed look.

Liliana sighed. "Oh, let me do it!"

She knelt down to help him, reaching for the rag. Immediately, the black goo flung itself to their touching hands and disappeared into their skin.

"What just happened?" Liliana asked, holding her hand out in front of her face.

A warm, tingling sensation spread up her arm.

Dante met her stare with a shocked expression. "I don't know, but I don't think it's anything good."

Chapter 8

Easy Remedies

Dante

Dante's arm felt like it was on fire. He didn't feel any different otherwise, but he didn't like the strange reaction he was having to the black goop. Burning wasn't usually a good sign.

"What was in that potion?" Liliana demanded, dark eyes furious.

"I wish I knew," he muttered.

Her eyebrows knitted together. "What do you mean? Didn't you brew it?"

He shook his head. "No. I... it was a gift from a friend. I never planned on using it... I didn't think... let's keep calm. I'm sure there's an easy remedy to this."

Liliana's face hardened. "What exactly does this *love* potion do?"

Dante flashed her an apologetic smile that felt more like a grimace. "I'm not sure. She only told me that it would lead me to my true match. But—"

"This isn't just a potion, Dante. Can't you feel it? There's a spell attached to it," Liliana cut him off, voice rising.

The use of his first name surprised him and would have made him smile if it weren't for the murderous glare that accompanied it.

"Well, now that you mention it, yes. I do feel it. A powerful spell, too. Huh."

Liliana growled in frustration. "Don't just stand there gawking! Do something. How do we break this... whatever this is?"

Dante frowned. "We could try a dividing spell?"

"Do you have all the ingredients for that?"

She looked around, her gaze snagging on her little sister, who watched silently with her hand over her mouth and watery eyes.

"It's alright, Ella," her voice softened.

"Let me grab something from the front," Dante said, heading for the door.

Pain shot through his arms and legs as he walked away. A heaviness followed, making it feel he was wading through the thickest mud.

"What are you doing?" Liliana asked behind him.

He turned to her. He'd only made it two steps. "I think it's the spell. I'm trying to leave."

"If this is some sort of prank, I swear..." Liliana said, letting her warning fade away.

Dante spread his arms with a huff. "I swear, I'm not trying to irk you. This is difficult. My legs won't listen."

He took a wide step, sucking in a breath at the pain that spread up his limbs. Pushing through the pain, he took another giant step. He was halfway to the door now.

"You look ridiculous," Liliana said behind him.

Dante glanced back to see her frown and Fiorella's amused smile she tried to cover with her hands.

He gave Liliana an annoyed look. "Let's see you try and move then."

R. L. Medina

With a snort, Liliana stepped toward him, one eyebrow raised.

"Well, of course, because you're moving closer to me," Dante said, taking another step toward the door.

The sharp pain returned, making his head throb with a dull ache. Dante grit his teeth and rushed to the door, gasping.

He put his hand on the knob and looked at Liliana. "How come you're not feeling the pain?"

She shrugged. "Maybe because I'm not the one trying to leave? Does this help?" she asked as she moved toward him.

The pain ebbed. He sighed in relief and nodded to her. Motioning for her to follow him, he opened the door and walked through. The door slammed shut behind him.

A jolt went through his body, making him bend over in pain.

"What are you doing?" he gasped out.

"I just wanted to see something," Liliana's voice called from the other side of the door. "Are you still in pain?"

Dante glared at the door. "Yes."

"I think I'm starting to feel it too."

"Wonderful. Now are you coming out to help me get the stuff for the spell?" Dante asked, his irritation bleeding through.

"Hold on. Maybe if we stay like this for a little while longer the pain will stop."

Before he could point out how foolish her plan was, his body leapt at the door, his head banging into the wood.

"What the..." His words were cut off as the magic threw him at the door once again.

"What are you doing? Stop it. You're scaring my sister," Liliana said sharply.

"I'm not doing this on purpose! Open the door, Liliana," Dante shouted as his body rammed itself against the door once more.

The door swung open, making him tumble forward and into the glaring witch.

She caught his fall, her touch sending a shock of awareness through him. The pain settling into something more manageable, Dante straightened and smoothed back his curls.

"Are you alright?" Liliana asked, a touch of amusement in her tone.

Dante glared at her and rubbed his forehead. "I just had my head slammed into the wood."

Liliana glared back at him. "I didn't tell you to run into the door repeatedly."

Feeling irritated himself, Dante scoffed. "You do realize it's the potion, don't you? You don't think I purposefully slammed myself into the door, do you? You could have opened the door the first time you heard me running into it."

Ignoring him, she turned to her sister. "Fiorella, can you take Fabrizio back home and get Mama? Bring some of the lilies from the garden."

Fiorella hesitated. "I'll just walk up the mountain. I'll be fast."

Liliana shook her head. "It would be faster with the wagon."

"But I've never driven it by myself before," Fiorella said, glancing embarrassedly at Dante.

Her sister sighed and nodded. "Okay, but please hurry. And bring my spell books too."

Fiorella nodded, glanced back at the little potted plant on the counter, and hurried past them to the door. The bell jingled behind her as she left the shop.

Dante stared at the curly-haired witch before him. Her eyes were dark and calculating, meeting his gaze.

"Well, this isn't quite what I'd envisioned when I told you we should work closely."

She gave him a flat look. Clearly, she was in no mood for

jokes. If he could have just gotten one smile out of her, he would have considered it a win.

"The division spell?" Liliana asked, pulling Dante out of his thoughts.

He cleared his throat and motioned for her to lead the way to the front. She waited for him to follow before moving forward. Together, they walked to the long, black-painted counter and shelves of product.

"This one should work. Though I have to warn you, it does leave a bitter taste for a few days," Dante said, grabbing a vial from the shelf behind the counter.

Liliana peered around him, squinting at the label. "That won't be strong enough. We need to know the ingredients of the potion and steps to the spell. Can you ask your... friend?"

"I can, but she's in the city. It will take a few days to get a letter to her and hear back."

Liliana groaned, rubbing her forehead. "Lovely."

"How was I supposed to know you and your sister would go nosing through my kitchen?"

Her brow furrowed. "We weren't nosing. We were dropping off the talismans I made for the Hallow's Eve."

"You could have left them on the front counter," Dante replied with his back to her.

He pulled down all the bottled spells and potions that might help them out of their predicament.

Liliana snorted, drawing his attention. He met her eyes.

"You were so busy flirting, I thought it would be best if we didn't disturb you."

Dante frowned. "I wasn't flirting. I was... making a sale."

She rolled her eyes and waved his words away. "Let's try one of these and see if it helps. You'll still have to write your friend though. As soon as possible. Why did she give you a love potion, anyway?"

Dante shrugged and glanced away. "It was just a nice gesture."

Liliana studied him and shook her head. "People don't give love potions as a nice gesture. She's probably some poor woman whose heart you've broken with your games."

A scoff escaped Dante. "I beg your pardon? I don't know what you've heard about me, but I assure you, I don't make it a habit to go around and break women's hearts."

"Your habits are none of my concern. Or at least they won't be as soon as we're free of this spell," Liliana muttered under her breath.

She picked up one of his vials and waved it at him. "Let's start with this one."

Following her lead, Dante grabbed the rest of the vials and jars to carry toward his kitchen. They set them on the little table and walked over to the sink to wash their hands.

"What is that thing?" Liliana asked pointing at the little potted plant.

"I'm not sure. I bought it from a peddler in the city before I left. They claimed it came from deep in the Youngfrou forest. Its leaves' secretion is supposed to have healing properties, but I haven't found that to be so."

Liliana frowned at it.

"Ready?" Dante asked, drying his hands on the towel.

Her eyes snapped to his. "Let's see what you can do."

Dante bit back the suggestive comment that came to mind, remembering his promise to Massimo. Things were strictly business.

After several vials of potions and spell attempts later, daylight was starting to fade, and they were still no closer to breaking the spell as they'd been before.

Dante slumped into the chair, leaning forward on his arms. His head throbbed from the effort. Liliana stood beside him, fanning herself in the heat of the kitchen. The fire roared from the hearth, warming Dante's cauldron for the next brew.

"Fiorella should be back any moment with the lilies for the breaking spell," Liliana said, wringing her hands together.

Dante groaned. "That's what you said before."

She frowned and opened her mouth to respond but was cut off by a loud shriek.

Her eyes widened. "*Santos!* What is that?"

Dante glanced up at his closed bedroom door. "She's starting to wake up."

Liliana gave him a sharp look. "She?"

Standing to his feet, Dante motioned for her to follow. Their footsteps echoed loudly in the silence as they walked to the room.

Dante opened the door and waved her in. Too tired and drained for another spell, he picked up the box of matches on the side table and pulled a match out to light the candles.

Liliana stood close beside him, the smell of her lavender soap surrounding him. Dim sunlight streamed in from the large window above his wide bed. In the corner of the room, Ometta nestled atop a large wooden post.

The golden glow from the now lit candles gave the room a soft, romantic air. Dante turned to watch Liliana as she took it all in. Her eyes roamed the sparse furniture, briefly snagging on his giant bed, before landing on Ometta.

She glanced at him. "Is that your... pet?"

At the sound of the witch's voice, Ometta looked up, blinking her large yellow eyes.

Liliana gasped.

"You have a familiar?" she asked, a touch of awe in her voice.

Dante smiled and met her questioning gaze. "Her name is Ometta."

The owl flew closer, its eyes fixed on Liliana. Landing with a loud thud on the side table and knocking the lamp over, she cocked her head at the witch and let out a high-pitched shriek. Dante waited for Liliana's reaction.

Unsurprisingly, she didn't flinch or gasp. Instead, her lips broke into a smile. It was the first genuine smile Dante had seen and, though it wasn't directed at him, he couldn't help but smile too.

"I think she likes you," Dante said, motioning Liliana closer.

"She's beautiful. I've never met a familiar before... Is this her only form?" Liliana asked, reaching a hand out to the owl.

Ometta looked to him.

Dante hesitated. "No, she has three forms. This one, a child's, and her true one. But she only shows that one to me."

Liliana's eyes snapped to his. She didn't say anything, but Dante couldn't help but feel that something had changed between them. Maybe she was beginning to see that he wasn't just the flirtatious peacock she'd branded him as.

She opened her mouth but was cut off by the sound of knocking. Muffled voices shouted from outside the store.

Dante frowned. "Who could that be making all that noise?"

Liliana shook her head ruefully. "My family."

Chapter 9

A Family Dinner

Liliana

"Did you all have to come?" Liliana asked as her mother and sisters filed into the shop, one by one.

"Yes," Alessia answered, followed by Massimo.

"Except for the elves. They're dining together at my villa tonight," she added as she handed Liliana a stack of her spell books.

Dante smiled at them, ushering them further into his shop. "Well, isn't this a lovely surprise. Do I smell something savory?"

Pamina grinned and held up the large, covered dish. "I brought some ravioli!"

She glanced at Liliana. "I thought you'd like some food and company while you're working."

Alessia turned to Liliana with a concerned look. "Is there anything we can do to help? Fiorella told us what happened."

The young girl flinched, staring down at the floor.

"It was just an accident. We're fine," Dante answered cheerfully, giving Fiorella a reassuring smile.

His eyes met Liliana's briefly before looking to Massimo.

"Though this does give us a good excuse to finally dine together, doesn't it?"

"Does this mean you two are in love now, or what?" Serafina asked, bluntly, an amused grin on her face.

Liliana shot her a glare. Before she could respond, Mama touched her shoulder and motioned her over to the corner of the room. Her brow furrowed as she inspected Liliana all over.

"Well? It's a strong spell, but it can be broken, right?" Liliana asked her as she set the books down on one of the empty shelves.

"Spells are... tricky. It would help to have the one who made it here. Maybe they could give us some clues as how to break it."

She brushed Liliana's curls back softly. "Are you really okay, *amore*? Tell me what you're feeling."

Liliana shrugged. "I feel the same. That's the strange part. I don't feel any different about him. The potion was meant to only show him his true match if he consumed it, but there was a spell hidden within it that once activated... Well, I'm not sure what it does, but I can't physically separate myself from his presence, at least not without severe pain."

"Hmm. Interesting," Mama said, dark eyes narrowed in calculation.

She glanced at Dante, who was chatting with Massimo. Liliana followed her gaze and huffed. Her mother better not be getting any ideas about playing matchmaker again.

"If you know a way to break this, you have to tell us, Mama."

Her mother's head whipped back to her. "I wish I could help, but I'm only a seer. Spells have never been my strength. Don't worry, *amore*. We'll figure this out. Most spells fade on their own anyway."

She gave Liliana a cheerful smile, looking much more optimistic than Liliana was feeling.

"Did you bring the lilies?" Liliana asked, glancing at her mother and sisters.

"Here they are," Fiorella answered, holding up a bouquet of fresh lilies to her.

Liliana took them, careful not to touch the petals. Lilies were a well-known way to break spells, but they were also poisonous in their natural form.

"We'll eat first and then we can see about this spell," Mama announced with a clap of her hands.

Dante hesitated. "As much as I'd love to dine here with all of you, I'm afraid my table only seats two."

Massimo grinned. "That's why I brought a table and some chairs in my wagon."

He motioned for Dante to follow him outside but paused. "Oh, wait. I'm sorry. I forgot you can't leave her presence." He glanced at Liliana.

"I can help!" Fiorella said, heading for the door.

Liliana sighed and set the lilies down in one of the empty baskets on the shelves. She turned to Dante. "I suppose, we should take a break now anyway."

He nodded in agreement, a weary look on his face. Even with the help of his familiar, they hadn't been able to weaken the spell, let alone break it.

Brushing her hands off on her dress, Liliana motioned for Dante to follow her to help the others bring in the wooden table and chairs. After several attempts and arguments of how they should do it, they finally managed to get the large table inside.

Signor Covelli, the baker next door, came out to see what the commotion was. Pamina gave him a friendly nod as she carried one of the chairs in. The older man waved in response, a curious look on his face as he watched them move the furniture in.

Liliana shook her head and glanced at Dante. "Great. Now we have the attention of your neighbors."

He smiled. "Maybe we should invite him in for supper?"

"Oh, that would be lovely. He's probably lonely living all alone," Pamina whispered before disappearing into the shop.

Dante turned toward the baker.

"No," Liliana said, grabbing Dante's arm.

A ripple of heat filled her at the contact. She released him at once and shook her head.

The last thing she wanted was for their curse to be known all over town. She could only imagine what they would say. That she was just like the others— falling for him. Giordana would have an absolute fit. A small smile spread on her face at the thought.

Dante, misreading her amusement, smiled back. His eyes reflected the glow of the streetlights around them. Night was growing dangerously close and the thought of having to spend it side by side with the handsome warlock made Liliana uneasy. The next spell they tried had better work.

Following the others, they made their way back to the kitchen. They'd moved the little table and chairs out to make room for the larger one, which now took up most of the room.

Serafina poked the fire in the hearth, the flames coming to life and filling the kitchen with a cozy warmth.

Pamina set out plates around the table while Mama and Alessia placed the silverware and napkins around. Massimo set the last chair down and Fiorella stood beside the little plant, touching its large leaves.

"Ella, don't," Liliana said, shaking her head.

Fiorella frowned. "Why? It's just a harmless baby plant." She looked over to Dante. "Does it have a name?"

Dante gaped at her, eyes darting from her to Liliana. "Uh.. no. Why don't you name it?"

Liliana shot him a look. Naming it would only make her sister grow more attached to the strange flower.

He shrugged at her glare and pulled out a chair for her to sit beside Alessia. Liliana bit back the sharp retort on her tongue and sank into the seat.

"How about Tito?" Fiorella asked, holding the little pot in her palm. She held it up for them all to see.

Dante smiled warmly at her, making the young girl blush. "I love it."

The others murmured their agreement as Pamina started plating the ravioli. A rich, savory smell filled the room, making Liliana's stomach rumble in anticipation. Her sister was the best cook and baker in Zamerra.

Friendly chatter echoed around the room, making Liliana squirm with impatience. She was stuck to the infuriating warlock by a powerful spell, unable to separate herself, and yet here her family came with dinner, acting as if everything was fine.

Feeling her mother's heavy stare, Liliana tried to school her features. She took a sip from the wine Pamina had placed in front of her, letting the magical drink do its work. The smooth, sweet liquid warmed her from the inside, settling her emotions.

Liliana sighed and looked up to see Dante staring at her from across the table. Her heart lurched. She glanced away, pushing away the strange feeling. It was just the spell at work, playing with her emotions.

Fiorella set the potted plant on the table and held up a forkful of ravioli to its mouth. It gobbled and slurped the food down noisily, leaves flapping in excitement.

Fiorella giggled. "Tito likes it!"

"Are you sure you should be feeding that thing like that?" Liliana asked as she watched.

Her sister stroked its petaled head and frowned. "Tito

needs to eat too. It's just a baby, Liliana. It needs someone to take care of it." She gave Dante a hopeful look.

He nodded, mouth full of pasta.

Alessia exchanged a worried glance with Liliana. Even Pamina and Serafina looked wary of the little pasta-eating plant.

"What if it grows bigger and develops an appetite for... meat?" Alessia asked.

"You mean flesh," Liliana muttered.

Fiorella gasped, holding Tito close to her chest "Don't say that! Tito wouldn't hurt anybody. I can help it learn."

She turned green eyes back on Dante. "My plant magic can help."

Before Liliana could step in, Dante smiled and waved a hand at the little plant. "That's wonderful. You should take it then. I don't have a use for it."

Fiorella squealed with delight. Serafina grinned, leaned over the table and handed Tito a piece of her bread. It gobbled it up greedily.

Liliana shot her mother a pointed look. Mama shrugged away her concern, as she always did, and smiled as Fiorella pet the plant's head.

Sighing, Liliana shook her head. It would have to be a problem for another day. She had enough to worry about for the time being.

"We should get back to work," Liliana said, setting down her empty bowl. It clanged loudly on the table.

Dante paused mid-bite and looked at her. "But I'm not even done eating yet."

"Maybe if you talked less..." she mumbled.

"You've already performed so many spells, amore. I think it's time to call it a night," Mama said softly, standing to her feet.

Liliana's eyes snapped to her. "Call it a night? What are we supposed to do? I can't stay here."

Dante frowned. "It's just for one night. I can't leave my shop unattended."

"Why not? It's just for one night," Liliana shot back.

He gave her a flat look and jerked his thumb toward the silver cauldron by the fire. "We still have to prepare the breaking spell. You really want to leave it unattended all night with no one around who can control it?"

Liliana groaned. He was right, though she hated to admit it. They couldn't leave while the spell was still forming. It needed at least several hours and that was after she crushed the lilies into the mixture.

"Don't worry, no one will know you're even here," Pamina said encouragingly as she stood to clear the dishes.

Alessia rose to help her, giving Liliana a sympathetic look. "We brought a cot and some bedding just in case..."

Liliana's gaze snapped to her. "Just in case? I'd expect this scheming from Mama, but now you too, Alessia?"

Her sister's face reddened as she glanced at the others. "I'm just trying to help, Liliana. Tell me, how I can help you?"

Feeling slightly guilty about her accusation, Liliana rubbed her forehead and sighed. "Make sure that letter gets to the post first thing in the morning. Please. If we can't break this ourselves, hopefully the witch who made it can."

Mama smiled. "I'm sure she can. Everything will be fine."

Gathering the others, she led them back to the front of the shop, their footsteps noisy against the wood.

Alessia stopped and leaned closer to Liliana. "We can stay with you, if you like. Massimo and I."

Liliana glanced at her fae brother-in-law and then back to her sister. He gave her an encouraging nod. "No. That's all right. We'll be fine."

A worried look flashed on her sister's face. "Are you sure?

Massimo has assured me that all will be well, that his friend is an honorable gentleman, but if you're worried—"

"I'm not. I'll be fine. I can take care of myself, Alessia," Liliana cut her off, feeling the warlock's gaze upon them.

Truthfully, she was more worried about what the spell would do to her. Could it turn her into some lovesick fool? In any case, she would be prepared. If it came to it, there were a few spells she could do to make sure she didn't do anything too... foolish.

She knew better than to fall for the flirtatious warlock.

After saying goodbye to her family, she watched from the window as the wagons pulled away. Silence echoed in the little shop, the cold night air swirling in after their departure. A shiver went up her back.

"Ready to finish setting up the potion for the spell?" Dante asked, handing her the basket of lilies she'd set aside.

Liliana took it and nodded at him.

They walked back to the kitchen and Dante placed the cauldron on top of the fire. Liliana glanced at the empty spot where Tito had sat. She didn't like Fiorella taking that thing home, but at least Pamina would keep an eye on it while she was away.

"Here. You do it," she said, shaking herself out of her thoughts. It was better if he did it with a clear mind than risk her emotions being entangled into the mixture.

Dante took the basket of lilies from her and chanted over them before dumping them all into the cauldron.

Liliana watched with interest as the ingredients boiled in the silver cauldron. The smell of lilies and fire filled the kitchen.

The warlock plucked a few strands of wool from his sweater and threw them in, before turning to face Liliana.

She ripped a button from the top of her dress and dropped it into the smoking cauldron.

"Well, now that that's set..." Dante said, pulling his sweater off over his head.

Liliana's eyes widened. "What are you doing?"

Dante gave her a strange look, folding the sweater in his hands. "Getting ready for bed."

Heat rushed across her skin. "You can't... you're not... dressed."

He looked down at his shirtless chest and back at her, eyebrow arched. "I'm not going to sleep in the same clothes I've worn all day. Are you?"

His gaze dipped down her dress, making Liliana flush.

"I'm not going to sleep at all. I'll sit out here and watch the spell," she answered quickly, avoiding looking at his toned chest.

Dante sighed. "You can't sit out here all night. Otherwise, I won't be able to leave the room or sleep."

Liliana shrugged. "You can sleep out here, on the cot my sister brought."

She motioned toward the bundled bedding on top of the large table her family had left.

"Or you could sleep in my bed, and I'll take the cot in my bedroom so we can both sleep comfortably," he said, frustration in his tone.

Liliana opened her mouth to argue, but stopped at the weary look he gave her.

"Please. It's just one night. Tomorrow we'll perform the breaking spell and this... will all be over," he said, voice tired.

Whether it was the love potion or spell at work, Liliana heard herself agree. "Fine. One night."

Chapter 10

The First Night

Dante

After opening the back door for Ometta to return from her nightly hunt, Dante turned to see Liliana watching him, hugging herself. A concerned look was painted on her face.

"What is it?" he asked.

Her brown eyes met his. "You should set a protective spell if you're going to leave the door open all night."

"Ometta is on duty. She'll be back in time to scare any intruder. Besides, I'm not some helpless sap," he added, puffing out his chest, which he'd covered with his flannel night shirt.

Liliana frowned. "Nor am I, but with Hallow's Eve approaching and this... spell we're under, I think we should take the extra precautions."

Dante groaned. The last thing he wanted to do was perform another spell. He ran his fingers through his curls and looked at her. "If you want to do it, go ahead. I'm going to sleep."

Eyes narrowed, she walked past him, hands raised in front of the open door. The cold night air blasted in, filling Dante's room with the smell of chimney smoke and autumn. Flames flickered from the candles on the dresser and walls.

Liliana stood, her back to him, her body trembling slightly.

"Wait," Dante reached from behind her, grabbing one of her hands.

The warm, electrifying touch of her skin made him suck in a breath. "You should let your body rest. I think we've both reached our limit of spells for the day."

Her nearness enveloped him, her dark curls tickling his chin. She smelled like smoke, with a hint of her lavender soap teasing him. A wave of desire rushed through him. He released her hand and stepped away before he did something foolish.

Chest rising slowly, Liliana turned to face him. "I think you're right. We should save all our energy for the breaking spell tomorrow."

In the warm glow of the candles, her features looked softer. Maybe all the work they'd done had snuffed out the fight out of her, or maybe the spell was starting to strengthen.

Your true match. The old witch's words echoed in Dante's mind.

"You can let go of my hand now," Liliana's words startled him.

He released her, his skin still tingling from the touch.

Liliana folded her arms around herself, shivering slightly. Dante pulled his plush, velvet robe off the bedpost and wrapped it around her shoulders.

"Thank you," she said softly, eyes dancing away from him.

Dante was at a loss for words. Something that was rare for him. He watched as the beautiful witch moved away and walked to his bed. She pulled the heavy wool blanket down and glanced at the cot on the floor beside the bed.

She looked at Dante. "Are you sure you don't want me to sleep on the cot? This is your bed after all..."

Finding his voice, Dante shook his head. "It's yours for tonight. I'll be fine on the floor. Trust me, I've slept in far worse."

Secretly, he'd hoped they could share the bed, but with the spell pulsing through him, it was probably best he stayed away.

"Now, I'm beginning to think the cot is a safer choice for me," Liliana said, glancing uncertainly at his large bed.

Dante snorted. "Let me assure you, you're the only woman who's been in my bed."

Her eyebrow arched in disbelief.

"It's a new bed," Dante added with a shrug.

Liliana looked away and sat down on his bed, bending down to unlace her boots. Dante watched as she pulled out her stockinged feet and climbed farther up the bed. She settled herself under the thick covers, her dark curls spilling out around her on the pillow.

Heat prickled his skin. When he'd envisioned her in his bed, this wasn't exactly what he had in mind. Just the sight of her laying there, under the heavy robe and blankets, dark eyes on him, was the most alluring thing he'd seen.

He turned away quickly, ignoring the questioning look on her face. It was the spell making him feel this way. Never mind that he'd been attracted to her before. This new sensation... it had to be the spell working its magic.

"Goodnight," Dante said softly, pulling himself out of his revelry as he walked over to the cot in the corner.

"Goodnight," she answered, turning away from him.

With a groan, Dante crawled under the quilts and tried to get the image of her out of his mind. How was he supposed to sleep with Liliana in his bed, a mere few feet away? What if the breaking spell didn't work and they were stuck together for good?

He shook the questions away. They had to find a way to break it before he did something stupid.

* * *

Something nudged Dante gently in the ribs. He woke with a groan, his body stiff and sore all over. He blinked against the bright sunlight streaming in from the window. When had he opened the curtains?

"Ah! You're finally awake. Good. Let's get started," Liliana's chipper voice startled him.

Dante closed his eyes and groaned again. "Oh, wonderful. You're a morning person."

Liliana frowned at him. "It's past breakfast."

"I didn't sleep well," his words came out as groggy as he felt.

She shrugged. "You can take a nap later, once we've broken this spell."

Dante gave her a flat look. "Normally, I'd find your determination admirable, but in this instance, I find it annoying."

Liliana snorted. "I'm annoying? I've been waiting for hours for you to wake up so I can leave this cursed room."

Sitting up, Dante rubbed his eyes and stifled a yawn. "I told you I couldn't sleep. This cot isn't nearly as comfortable as it looks."

"Well, I offered to sleep there."

Dante shivered in the morning cold. He glanced at the wooden post where Ometta sat, curled up and sleeping. The back door was shut now, but the room was freezing.

"There's caffé in the kitchen. And once you get up and move, I can rekindle the fire," Liliana said, sounding like a mother trying to coax a difficult child.

"My, you're eager this morning, aren't you," Dante replied, brushing his curls out of his face.

He didn't consider himself a vain person, but the fact that Liliana was seeing him in such a poor state made him frown.

"Pamina left honey cakes, too."

Dante's head snapped to her. "Ah. You should have started with that."

He pushed the heavy quilt off and stood to stretch. A yawn escaped him as he followed Liliana into the kitchen. The fire in the hearth was dying, the spell they'd place to keep it lit all night finally fading. The room smelled like burnt leaves and ash.

"Where are the cakes?" Dante asked as Liliana walked over to the cauldron.

She turned to him with a frown. "How can you think about food before we've even checked the potion?"

"I work better with a full belly."

"Hurry and eat then. I want to get this potion finished so we can begin the spell." Liliana said, pointing to a wrapped-up plate on the kitchen counter.

After pouring himself a steaming cup of caffé, he trudged over to the honey cakes and snatched one from the plate.

"These are even better than the bakery's next door," Dante murmured with a mouthful of the delicious pastry.

He closed his eyes and savored the sweet, spongy treat.

"Pamina has baking magic," Liliana answered with a shrug.

"She should open her own bakery. She'd make a fortune."

Liliana turned to him, hand on her hip. "There are other things to pursue than fortune,"

Dante licked the sticky honey from his fingers and met her gaze. "Oh, I know. I've chased them all."

Before she could respond, a loud rap sounded on the door in the front of the shop.

Her eyes bulged. "Don't make a sound. Maybe they'll leave."

Dante glanced down at his flannel shirt and loose trousers. "Won't it look more suspicious if we don't open the shop?"

"No. You could be ill. How would they know?"

"Hello! Signor Lazzaro? I know you're there. I saw your wagon and horse in the stable."

Dante gave Liliana a pointed look. She motioned for him to be quiet.

"Signore, if you don't open the door, I'll assume the worst has befallen you and will have Patrizio come right away."

Dante shot Liliana an incredulous look. Was the man serious? If they really didn't open, the townsfolk would burst in just like that?

Liliana bit her lip and nodded, waving him back into the bedroom.

"Get dressed. The sooner you satisfy his nosiness, the sooner he'll leave us alone. Just tell him... you are brewing more tonics and need the day to prepare."

Dante pulled a fresh sweater out of his drawer and started to strip. Liliana's gaze snagged on his bare chest, making him grin.

Caught looking, she turned her back to him with a huff. "Hurry up."

Grabbing her woolen shawl from the bedpost, she draped it over her shoulders and pulled it tight across her chest, hiding her missing top button.

More knocking came from the front, the voice now muffled.

"Persistent, isn't he?" Dante murmured as he slicked back his curls in the little mirror on the wall.

"It's Signor Marcello."

"Ah. Yes. The pharmacist. I met him yesterday."

Dante turned to her with a bow. "Let's get this over with, then."

Together, they walked through the kitchen and into the front of the shop. Dante drew back the curtains and opened the door for the man.

Signor Marcello's eyes widened on them, darting from Dante to Liliana.

"Good morning, Signor!" Dante greeted cheerfully.

The man grunted. "What is she doing here?"

Dante grinned. "Signorina Silveri? She's my assist—er, business partner?" he backpedaled after a glance at Liliana's scowl.

The older man grunted again, bushy brow furrowed in annoyance. "Oh, I see what's going on here."

Dante and Liliana exchanged curious looks.

"You do?" Dante asked him.

"I'm not a fool. You two are forming an alliance to push me out of business. Well, it won't work. My family has been here since the Zamerra was founded and everyone is loyal to me," He said with a snarl, waving a finger at them as he spoke.

Liliana snorted behind Dante.

The man's eyes darted to her, face reddening. "I've been more than fair, allowing you to sell your potions, but now you've gone too far. You... you witch!"

Dante's hackles rose at the venom directed at Liliana. This he would not allow.

He stepped forward, towering over the man. "You say that as if it's an insult. I'd be very careful if I were you, Signore. Your family may have the loyalty of the town, but you would do well to remember who *her* family is."

His voice lowered, his words laced with warning. If Massimo, as the count, didn't deal with the big mouthed *asino*, he would.

Flustered, Signor Marcello gaped at him.

"Now, as much as I'd love to stay and chat, we are very

busy. The shop is closed for the day, Signore, so that we can properly prepare some more tonics. Come back another day, and I'll be able to help you with all your needs," Dante prattled off, waving the man away.

The pharmacist's face was mottled red and white. "I don't need anything from your shop! I—"

Dante shut the door in his face and locked it with a quick chant. He waved goodbye from the window before closing the curtains once more.

He turned back to Liliana, who stared at him with a strange look. "You didn't have to rise to my defense, you know. I'm perfectly capable of—"

"Taking care of yourself. I know, but I'm sure that wasn't the last we've seen of him. I'll let you tell him off the next time. You do have a way with words," Dante said, cutting her off.

They stared at each other for a moment, the bubbling cauldron in the kitchen loud in the silence.

As if snapping herself out of a spell, Liliana turned away first and headed for the back room.

She stood over the cauldron. "It's ready."

Dante frowned, unable to hide his disappointment. Funny, they'd been working so hard to free themselves, but the thought of it now left a bitter taste in his mouth.

He shook the thoughts from his mind. The sooner the love spell was broken, the sooner he could return to his usual self. Any more time spent with Liliana, and he feared he'd lose sight of what was most important. His magic. His freedom.

"We should do the chant together. Make sure there are no weak spots," Liliana's words brought him back to the present.

Dante grinned. "I'll cover your weak spots if you cover mine."

She rolled her eyes. "Come on. Let's do it."

Dante's grin widened, but before he could make another

comment, Liliana silenced him with a dark look. She ladled the brown goo into a large wooden bowl and blew on it.

"One more honey cake first." He gave her a placating smile.

He shoved one into his mouth and washed it down with the last of his caffé.

Wiping the sticky residue of the honey cake from his fingers with a wet cloth, Dante nodded. "Yes, alright. Let's get on with it. Are you ready?"

She nodded, handing him the bowl of smoky smelling potion. Dante took it in his hands and chanted a quick cooling spell. The steam evaporated instantly.

He drank the bowl half gone, coughing as the warm liquid burned his throat. His eyes grew watery, and his nose started running as he gave it to Liliana.

Attractive.

Liliana downed the rest of the liquid, swallowing hard.

"How come your eyes didn't water?" Dante asked with a touch of annoyance.

She ignored him and set the empty bowl down on the table. Her brow furrowed in concentration as she read from one of the spell books she'd brought.

"No need for books. I have the spell memorized," Dante said.

A flash of annoyance crossed her face. "So do I, but I just want to make sure we didn't forget anything. Can't be too careful."

Dante grunted, holding his tongue. Tearing her eyes away from the book and back to him, Liliana lifted her hands toward his.

He moved closer, lifting his hands in the same manner. Their fingers touched first, then their palms. Warmth spread down his arms at the contact. Her hands were smaller than his and soft like silk. Awareness rippled through Dante, his body moving closer as if by instinct.

The smoke on her clothes and the lavender soap scent teased his nose, the smell both intoxicating and calming. Warm brown eyes peered up at him from long, dark lashes. Dante's gaze flickered to her slightly parted lips.

He had the irresistible urge to kiss them.

"Ready?" She asked, her voice sounding breathless.

Dante clenched his jaw, doing his best to ignore his desire. With a firm nod, he closed his eyes and began chanting. Liliana joined him, her voice echoing his.

Magic surged between them, filling the air with its electrifying sensation. Ringing filled Dante's ears as they recited the spell together, pain spearing through his temple.

He opened his eyes to find Liliana staring at him. Her blank expression was hard to read, but at least it wasn't the disgusted scowl she normally gave him.

"Did it work?" Dante asked, his words coming out thick and slow.

Liliana's gaze darted away. "I don't know. Let's see."

She withdrew her hands, breaking the tension. Dante lowered his arms as well and tried to shake off the sensation.

"I'll try and leave this time," Liliana said, backing towards the door slowly.

Her boots echoed loudly in the silence. Dante watched her go, waiting for the spell to react. Nothing happened. The pull he'd felt earlier was gone.

Liliana sighed loudly. "We did it. Thankfully. I'm glad that's over. What a nightmare that would have been."

"It would have been quite the thing to explain to everyone though, wouldn't it?" he added with a smirk.

Her eyes snapped to his, an unreadable look on her face.

She made it to the doorway and paused. "Have a good day, Signore."

"Really? After all that, you still can't call me Dante? We did spend the night together, after all."

Ignoring him, she disappeared into the front, leaving Dante alone in the little kitchen. He listened as she left the shop, disappointment filling him.

Chapter 11

The Fairy Gate

Liliana

Liliana sighed, her breath puffing into the chilly air. The smell of just brewed caffé and freshly baked bread filled her lungs. After the night and morning, she'd had, she was more than ready to get home and pour herself a giant cup of Pamina's special brew. She'd barely slept.

The image of Dante standing shirtless in his room sprang to her mind. The warm glow of the candles. His toned chest. The small patch of soft-looking chest hair. His deep brown eyes.

Pushing the images away, Liliana made her way down the street and past the growing crowd. Thankfully, the townsfolk were too busy with their own Hallow's Eve preparations to notice her leaving the warlock's apothecary. Voices blurred together as wagon wheels echoed across the cobblestone streets.

Some of the shopkeepers were outside, stringing garland of dried leaves and berries over their windows. They were festive decorations, but they would do nothing to stop the spirits that would be released on Hallow's Eve.

Liliana squared her shoulders back. There was still much

left to do and not much time left to do it. Now that they were free of the horrible spell, she could get back to work.

Halfway up the mountain to her villa, pain struck her hard between the eyes.

Liliana gasped, a hand flying to her forehead. Dizziness swept over her.

No. No. No.

The spell was back. Stronger than ever.

After a painful march back through town, Liliana made it to the apothecary, seething.

Before she could knock, the door swung open.

Dante blinked in surprise at her. "You felt it too?"

"What have you done now?" Liliana asked as she stormed past him into the shop.

Dante gaped at her. "Me?"

"We need to break this. Now. We'll stay up all night tonight if we need to, but this is unacceptable," Liliana said.

"All night?" Dante asked, eyebrows raised.

She folded her arms across her chest and met his stare. "Why? You have special plans for tonight?"

The image of him with Giordana flashed in her mind, making her scowl.

Dante shook his head at her. "Well, I was invited to dinner. To your neighbor's villa."

Salvatore and Adriano's invitation. Liliana cursed inwardly, rubbing her forehead. She'd forgotten about it.

"Then we'll have to be quick about this. We need to get out of this mess you've put us in."

"I put us in? How is this my fault now?"

Liliana waved a hand to silence him, pacing the floor to think.

"Do you have to walk while you scheme?" Dante asked.

She continued, ignoring him, racking her brain for a solution. The breaking spell hadn't worked. Well, it had worked for a little while. She looked around for a clock and tried to count the minutes in her head. Nearly half an hour. Would it work again for another half hour?

Dante groaned. "This is starting to get annoying. Can't you sit while you think? Must you pace?"

Liliana threw him a dark look and shook her head. "If you don't have anything helpful to say, keep it to yourself."

"You could say please," Dante muttered.

"What did she put in that spell?" Liliana mused aloud.

"I don't know, but it was sneaky. Sneaky and brilliant. I only wish I hadn't been the target," Dante replied.

Coming to a stop in the middle of the room, Liliana turned to him. "We could try a different breaking spell? See if that would last?"

"Because this one worked so well."

She let out a frustrated breath. "Well, what do you suggest then? We can't just wait for your friend's instructions. I have things to do."

Dante frowned. "So do I. Do you think I want to be stuck like this?"

"Then let's try it again," she insisted.

"What about the Hallow's Eve preparations?" he asked.

"What about them?"

Dante gestured between them. "If we keep spending all our energy trying to break this spell, we won't have everything ready in time. Before you argue, I want to get out of this just as badly as you do, but until Signora Gavella writes back, we'll be wasting our time and efforts on more failed attempts."

He gave her a hesitant smile. "This ruse works for now, doesn't it? The townsfolk are none the wiser and perhaps, while we're preparing, something will spring to mind. Besides, most spells fade on their own. We just have to wait this out."

A harsh laugh escaped her. "So, your brilliant plan is to do nothing and ignore it. Carry on with business as usual? Some spells fade but how do we know this one isn't permanent?"

Dante frowned. "I doubt Signora Gavella would have given me a permanent spell. And what you've suggested hasn't worked. I'm not saying we do nothing, just that we should focus on the Hallow's Eve preparation for now."

Liliana sighed and folded her arms across her chest.

No. She couldn't take being stuck with him any longer. His infuriating smile. That infectious laugh. His penetrating gaze. The spell was playing with her emotions. This was dangerous.

"I do need to finish closing that Fairy portal," she admitted with another sigh.

Dante grinned and nodded. "Yes. We can do it together. Today."

"First, I need to stop home," she replied.

Hopefully, no one would be there.

After a quick stop inside her villa (that to her relief was empty) to change, Liliana carried a steaming mug with her as they headed for the woods. She sipped the warm liquid, letting her sister's magic wash over her.

Leaves crunched beneath their boots as they walked through the forest. Liliana's breath puffed out in the chilly air. She glanced in the direction of her home, envisioning a giant bowl of Pamina's hearty soup. Once they were done with the portal maybe they could stop back in for a quick lunch. Though the thought of running into her mother and sisters, back from wherever they'd been, made her nose wrinkle.

They'd have questions and comments. Mama would meddle.

"Are you going to do the honors or should I?" Dante's deep voice pulled her out of her thoughts.

The Fairy gate stood before them. Its magic was dormant, as usual, but Liliana wasn't taking any chances. Not with Hallow's Eve coming.

She turned to meet the warlock's stare. "I think we should both do it. It will go faster if we combine our magic."

Dante smirked. "You don't need to come up with an excuse to hold my hand, you know."

Liliana huffed. "Is everything amusing to you? Have you ever been serious about anything in your life?"

"Life is too short not to find the amusement in it. You take everything too seriously."

Irritation filled her at his words. He thought himself so much better than her.

"Some of us have had to work for everything we have," she snapped.

He looked taken aback. "Are you saying I haven't worked for what I have?"

"Not as hard as I have," she said with a shrug.

His nostrils flared. "That's a bold statement. You hardly know me or my work."

Liliana's eyebrow arched. "You make beauty potions. That's not that hard."

The warlock stopped suddenly, jaw clenching. "And sleeping tonics are harder?"

Heat rushed across Liliana's face. "At least I try to help people with serious problems. Not give them pretty powder for their wrinkles and warts."

"Oh! And you think I'm arrogant? That's ironic now, isn't it?"

Liliana met his glare, chest rising in fury. Mug now empty, she waved it in the air between them. "You are arrogant. And vain. And... and..."

Dante took a step toward her, closing the distance. His musky smell wrapped around her, warmth radiating from his body. The fiery look in his eyes made Liliana freeze. He didn't look angry anymore. He looked like he wanted to kiss her.

His words from the wedding replayed in her mind.

Turning away quickly, Liliana knelt beside the mushrooms and set down her mug. She raised her hands into the air and focused on the closing spell. Her heart hammered loudly in her ears. Her pulse raced. She closed her eyes and took a deep breath, trying to ignore his presence.

The spell was stirring something dangerous inside of her and she didn't like it. She didn't like it one bit.

Finishing the chant in her head, she took another deep breath and rose slowly.

Heart still racing, Liliana turned to Dante. He met her gaze with a contrite look on his face.

"I'm sorry," they said in unison.

Dante shook his head, "I shouldn't have spoken so sharply with you. I admire your work. Truly. I think you are very skilled. And to have learned so much independently, it really is admirable."

Liliana shifted uncomfortably under his compliments. He was challenging her first impression of him, and she didn't know how to reconcile it. Why couldn't he go back to being the annoying flirt she knew him as?

"Thank you. I think you are... skilled as well," she finally replied.

Brushing invisible dirt off her dress, she started walking back to the wagon they'd left on the road. Dante followed her.

"Now that that's done, we should make sure the town is

secure. Hopefully, the letter you wrote reaches your friend quickly. If I have to endure this *love* spell for any longer..."

"Would being stuck with me really be that awful?" Dante asked softly.

There was no hint of lightness or amusement in his tone now. Only vulnerability. Liliana wanted to say yes. *Yes, it would be the worst.* But he didn't deserve that and, if she were being honest, he was starting to grow on her.

"We should get back," she said instead, walking faster.

She was tempted to write her own letter to Dante's mentor, to give the woman a piece of her mind. The spell was not only insufferable, but it had struck at the most inconvenient time.

Hallow's Eve. What would happen if they couldn't break the spell before then?

"It's a little too quiet out here, don't you think?" Dante asked, pulling her from her thoughts.

She turned to look at the warlock.

"I don't like it," he added with a frown.

Liliana's lips quirked into a smile. "What's wrong with quiet? I like it. You should try it every once in a while. It's peaceful."

He gave her a side-eyed glance. "I'll indulge you if you indulge me," a grin spread on his face, "I mean that in the most respectable, innocent way, of course."

"Of course," Liliana said with a grunt.

"I'll be quiet if you tell me something I don't know."

"Something you don't know? We'll be at it all day then."

Dante made a face at her quip. "You're hilarious. I mean about you. Tell me something about yourself. Something that would shock me."

"I doubt there's anything left in the world that would shock you."

"Well, try. Please?"

She didn't know what to say. There was nothing special about herself to share. Nothing that he didn't already know. Liliana didn't know whether to be relieved or embarrassed by this.

"Alright, maybe that's too much. What about a memory? A favorite childhood memory?" Dante asked, glancing around the forest.

His head whipped back to her. "A memory in this forest. Surely, you have some good ones."

Liliana smiled in spite of herself. Images flashed in her mind. She and her younger sisters running wild and barefoot among the trees. Alessia chasing after them with their boots, worried they would injure themselves.

"I didn't always live here, you know. We came when I was twelve. One day when we were older, we discovered the Fairy portal. It was the same day I discovered my magic. Fiorella was just a toddler. She was the one, actually, who discovered the Fairy gate. Activated it. It nearly sucked her in, too."

Liliana stopped walking, lost in her memories. "I still don't know how I did it, but I closed the portal, all on my own. It took me a week to recover from that spell."

She shook her head. "I know that doesn't sound like a good memory, but that feeling when I discovered my magic. It was..."

"Unlike anything you'd ever felt before?" Dante finished for her with a knowing smile.

His eyes bore into hers. "That story does sound happy. Much happier than my childhood."

Liliana looked at him in surprise. A sudden curiosity filled her. What was Dante like as a child? It occurred to her that she didn't know anything about his past nor his family.

At her questioning look, he continued. "Like Massimo, I was an only child. My parents... they had a lot of expectations. Especially my father. He'd worked himself to the bone to get where we were, but it wasn't enough for him. He wanted me to push myself harder. More wealth. More power."

He turned to Liliana with a bitter smile. "I was a disappointment to him. He wanted me to move south and go into the Ministry of Magic. Can you imagine me on that stuffy board? Wearing those ghastly wigs and robes?"

Dante shuddered. "I'd rather be turned into a toad. Anyways, when my mother died, he cut me off. The only reason I was able to finish my studies was because I started making and selling my own potions. I even named my business after my father. Lazzaro and Son's."

He gave a short laugh, shaking his head. "Sorry. You don't want to hear my boring life story."

Liliana didn't know what to say. The harsh words she'd spoken earlier echoed in her mind. She'd been wrong to judge him.

"Your father sounds like a lovely man. I think he and Signor Marcello would get along quite nicely."

Dante snorted, a smile lighting his face and making her heart flutter. She preferred happy, teasing Dante to the sad image he'd painted of a struggling, young warlock with no family.

Suddenly growing serious, Dante reached for her hand. His touch spread a warmth up her arm. "Liliana, I..."

"Look!" a voice cut him off, echoing through the forest.

They turned to see Fiorella and Serafina running toward them. For once, Liliana was thankful for their intrusion.

Chapter 12

Stew for Two

Dante

D ante moved away from Liliana as her sisters greeted her with giant hugs. He bowed to them in greeting as they turned to look at him.

Fiorella pulled a familiar looking plant out of her pocket and held it up for him. "Look! Tito is growing."

Liliana frowned. "Already? That can't be good, Ella. What have you been feeding it?"

Serafina snorted. "Everything."

The little plant swiveled its odd-looking 'head' to Dante. It did look a little taller.

"What are you two doing in the woods?" Serafina asked, glancing between Dante and her sister.

"What are *you* two doing in the woods?" Liliana parroted back to her.

"I'm showing Tito around the forest," Fiorella answered, petting the plant's petaled head.

Liliana shot Dante an accusatory look. He got the impression she wasn't happy with him giving the plant to her sister,

99

but he couldn't see why. It was a harmless healing flower. What could possibly happen?

"We stopped into town to see how you were doing, but you weren't there. Didn't you do the breaking spell?" Serafina asked, dark eyes narrowing on them.

"Yes, but it only worked for a little while. Did Alessia send out that letter?" Liliana asked.

"I guess," Serafina answered with a shrug.

Liliana scoffed at her unhelpfulness and turned to Dante. "We should get back to town and finish the Hallow's Eve preparations."

Fiorella frowned. "But Pamina made stew. Mama will be upset if you don't come in and eat with us."

"Stew does sound delicious," Dante said, patting his stomach.

Liliana turned a fierce glare on him.

"Or not. Never mind. I forgot I hate stew," he added quickly.

Serafina chortled and gave her older sister a smirk. "You know you can't perform spells on an empty stomach, and you can't cook, Liliana."

Liliana huffed. "I can too cook."

Serafina made a face. "The only thing you're good at cooking is potions."

Before Liliana could reply, she darted back toward their villa. "I'll go tell Mama and Pamina you're coming."

"Wait! We have to get the cart and horse," Liliana called after her.

"Serafina already brought it to our villa. We saw it on the road," Fiorella answered.

She had remained behind, her gaze still fixed on Dante. He met her eyes and smiled. She looked away embarrassed.

Tucking Tito back into her dress pocket, she turned to chase after Serafina. Their steps echoed through the trees.

"Your sisters are quite amusing," Dante said, glancing at Liliana.

She snorted and shook her head. "That's one way of putting it."

"I can cook, you know. But she's right that we should eat something before we finish the work," Liliana added, a slight flush to her cheeks.

"I'm sure you're an excellent cook." Dante grinned and motioned for her to lead the way.

They walked in silence, taking in the autumn foliage above them. In the distance, squirrels chattered, and birds squawked. A cool breeze swept through the trees, rustling the leaves. The trees thinned as they walked and the noises faded.

"Do you hear anything? Voices?" Liliana asked, interrupting the quiet.

Dante turned to her in surprise. "Voices? You mean besides ours?"

She gave him an exasperated look. "The forest. Fiorella used to hear it calling to her. My mother helped me smother her power when she was younger. Just a little bit. Enough to leave her with some magic, but not too much. But lately, she's been hearing the voices again."

A warmth spread inside Dante. The fact that Liliana was trusting him with this knowledge made his chest swell.

"Well?" She asked, eyes expectant.

"Right, well, perhaps she's hearing the animals? She could have the same magic as Serafina."

"No. It's not that. I think it's related to the portal. She's the only one with the power to activate it once more. On this side, anyway."

Dante nodded in thought. "But you can close it. Like you just did now."

She paused and met his gaze. "Yes, but that's because it's dormant. If it's activated again... I don't think I could. Not like the first time, when I was a girl. That was a fluke. A young witch with no control unleashing all her power."

"Well, it's dormant and closed now, but should it come back to life, I'm here now. And with both of us together, I think we can manage," Dante said, giving her a reassuring smile.

Liliana smiled back, making his heart leap into his throat. He had the sudden urge to lean over and kiss her. To taste her lips. Pull her close against him and...

"Get ready for a lot of noise," Liliana said, breaking his thoughts.

Before he could ask her what she meant, a cacophony of meows and sharp barks filled the air. Liliana gestured to the short wooden gate before them. It was covered with so many vines and flowers, still in bloom, that he had missed it at first.

Liliana unlatched the gate and swung it open. The cats and Gio descended upon them, the noise almost deafening.

"I warned you!" Liliana shouted over their cries, leading him through the crowd of animals.

Dante followed her, careful not to step on any tiny paws, as they made their way through the yard. Plants of all various sizes, shapes, and colors took up most of the space. Unlike the rest of the area, the plants in their yard were still green and thriving. Its own little magical oasis.

The cats pressed them on all sides despite Liliana's attempts to shoo them. Serafina came to their rescue, sending the animals away with a wave of her hand.

"Some people have one or two guard dogs. I see you've opted for a dozen feral cats instead," Dante joked.

Serafina grinned at him. "There are seventeen cats and Gio is the best guard dog in the world."

She nodded in the little dog's direction. His tail wagged happily, head lifted at her compliment and big, bugged eyes fixed on Dante.

"So, I see," the warlock said, giving Liliana an amused look.

"Signor Lazzaro! Liliana! Come in," Liliana's mother called from the back door, waving to them.

Dante tipped his hat in greeting to her. "Thank you, Signora. I appreciate your hospitality."

She ushered them in and shut the kitchen door behind them. The heavenly aroma of stew made Dante's mouth water. Fire blazed from the hearth, filling the room with its cozy warmth. Pamina looked up and smiled at him in greeting, as she ladled stew into a bowl and handed it to Fiorella.

"Please, sit, Signore," Signora Silveri said, motioning for Dante to take a seat at the table.

"How are you?" She asked Liliana, pulling her aside.

Dante sank into the wooden chair and nodded in appreciation as Fiorella set the bowl in front of him.

He waited, pretending not to listen to Liliana's conversation, as the other girls sat down beside him. Pamina scooped some stew into a tiny bowl and placed it on the floor in front of the pantry.

Two little hands appeared, taking the soup, and disappearing back into the pantry.

Noticing his stare, Pamina gave him an apologetic look. "Our house elf, Bruno. He's a little shy around new people," she explained as she sat down with her own bowl.

Dante nodded in understanding. "Yes. House elves can be skittish."

"Do you have a house elf?" Serafina asked with a mouthful of bread.

Pamina gave her pointed look. "At least swallow first, Fina. Please. We have company," she flashed Dante an embarrassed look.

Dante bit back his amusement and shook his head. "No, but Massimo used to have one."

"Ruella! He told us about her," Fiorella said excitedly.

Serafina tore off another piece of her bread and waved it as she talked. "Do you have any children, Signore?"

Pamina made a choking noise.

"Fina!" Liliana exclaimed.

She and her mother joined them at the table, shooting disapproving looks at Serafina, who popped the bread into her mouth with a shrug.

Dante met Liliana's gaze. "No. No children."

She looked away and sat in her chair, across from him. Signora Silveri gave Dante a shrewd look, dark eyes narrowed. He shifted under her scrutiny and turned his attention to his stew. The savory broth warmed his throat.

"Are you coming to dinner tonight at the Rossi's villa?" Pamina asked, breaking the awkward silence.

Dante glanced at Liliana. A worried look crossed her face.

"I suppose it's too late to get out of it now. We have more work to finish first, but yes, we'll have to go," she said, giving Dante a miserable look.

"Is their cook that bad?" he asked in jest.

Liliana shook her head. "No, but we'll have to keep up the ruse. That we're... business partners."

She turned a glare on Serafina. "Absolutely no word is to be spoken about the love potion or spell."

Her sister rolled her eyes in response. "Yes, I know. Mama already told us we can't tell anyone."

"That includes Angelo," Liliana added with a pointed look.

Serafina gaped at her. "What? Why would I tell him? I don't even talk to him!"

Fiorella giggled, quickly turning away to feed Tito, at Serafina's dark look.

Liliana only shrugged, a small smirk on her face.

Dante watched their exchange with amusement. He liked seeing Liliana's sisterly side. It was clear she would do anything for her family. For the ones she loved. A strange yearning filled him at the thought.

"Massimo said you two were working on putting the safeguards up for the masquerade. Do you need any help with that?" Their mother asked, pulling Dante from his thoughts.

He looked to Liliana to answer.

She frowned at her mother's offer. "It's just setting barriers and handing out talismans for everyone to wear. I think we'll be fine but thank you."

"Do you have your costume yet for the masquerade, Signore?" Fiorella asked him.

Dante smiled. "I do, actually. I ordered a new suit before I left Delle Rose. It arrived when I got here."

"Ooh! What is it?" Serafina asked.

He waved his finger at her. "That's not how masquerades work, signorina. You're not supposed to know who is behind the mask. You're supposed to guess."

She frowned and turned to Liliana. "Have you even started on your costume? It's only five days away."

Liliana shot her an incredulous look. "No. I've been a little busy protecting everyone from the spirits and..." she motioned between her and Dante, "dealing with this..."

"This unexpected delight?" Dante offered, eyebrow arched.

"Don't worry! Mama and I will have your costume sorted," Pamina said with a cheerful smile.

A snort escaped Liliana. "As long as you don't make me into anything ridiculous."

Serafina smiled wickedly. "Like a peacock?"

Liliana's head snapped to Serafina. "Absolutely not."

"Hold on now, what's wrong with a peacock?" Dante asked, giving her an affronted look.

Instead of answering him, she stood to her feet, chair scraping the floor as she did.

"We need to get back to work," she said, motioning for Dante to stand up.

Sighing, Dante nodded and rose to his feet as well. He carried his bowl and spoon to the sink. Before he could turn on the water, Pamina was there, taking the dishes from his hands.

"I can do it, Signore."

"Oh. Thank you. And thank you for that lovely lunch. It was delicious."

"I thought you hated stew," Serafina said behind them with a teasing tone.

Dante smiled at her. "Not your sister's."

Pamina flushed and nodded at him in response. Saying goodbye to Liliana's family, they made their way outside to where their cart waited.

Dante helped Liliana into the wagon. Warmth spread through him at the contact. Her nearness made him dizzy. It was the spell at work. Was she feeling it too?

He pushed away the thoughts and glanced at her.

"Massimo said he would have the Patrizio hand out the talismans to the townsfolk. That should save us some time," Dante said as they started moving.

Liliana turned to him. "Yes, and we can bring two to dinner tonight for my neighbors."

"And your family," Dante said with a nod.

"I already made some for them," Liliana replied.

"And Massimo?"

She nodded. "Of course. He's family, too."

A wistfulness filled Dante. He was happy for his friend, marrying into such a warm and welcoming family, but he couldn't help but feel a little left out. Once the spell was broken and he and Liliana were free of each other, would he still be invited over for random lunches and walks in the forest?

Pushing the disappointment away, he tried to focus on the task at hand. It was better that way. No matter how kind they were to him, he knew he couldn't truly be a part of their family. He'd only disappoint them. Just as he had his own.

The rest of the drive back to town was quiet. Strangely, Dante didn't mind it. Not with Liliana pressed close beside him, her breath puffing out before her in the cold. She seemed to be lost in thought. Dante wondered what she was thinking about. Was she still so desperate to be rid of the spell, to be rid of him?

Chapter 13

Dinner Date

Liliana

Smoke filled Dante's kitchen, making Lilliana's eyes and throat sting. She coughed and motioned for him to open the window. They'd attempted another breaking spell, but something had gone wrong.

"Fantastic. Now all of Zamerra will come running, thinking your shop is on fire," she said, voice hoarse.

Dante waved the smoke toward the window and gave her a rueful smile. "Well, it's not quite the advertisement I'd hoped for, but I'll take it."

She groaned and blinked, trying to clear her eyes. A cough racked her body.

"We should get ready for dinner now. It's getting late," Dante said.

Dinner. With her family and their friends. What if they suspected something? What if her sisters spilled everything to them? Salvatore had loose lips and, even though she trusted him with some things, this was not one of them.

"Yes. We just have to make it through tonight," Liliana said with a heavy sigh.

"It's just dinner. With your family. And your neighbors. What could go wrong?" Dante flashed her a smile.

She rubbed her forehead. "Everything."

Turning to look at the talismans they'd finished, she nodded to herself. Though the necklaces were made crudely made with twine and spelled acorns, they would keep everyone safe from possession.

Once the barriers were in place and the talismans were handed out, they'd be ready. Breaking the love spell would have to wait until after the masquerade. Which meant four more nights with Dante.

"Well, did you want to wash up and change first or...?" The warlock's deep voice stirred her out of her thoughts.

Liliana looked down at her cotton dress. "I didn't bring another dress. I'll just have to go smelling like smoke."

Dante's eyes traveled down her length, making her skin heat. His dark eyes met hers. "Or you could use one of my anti-smelling powders. I have one in lavender. Like your soap."

Liliana gaped at him, his words surprising her. Was her soap that strong that he could smell it over all the smoke?

"Oh. Thank you," she answered, accepting the tin can of powder he held out to her.

"The breaking spell from this morning should still be active. At least for half an hour like before? You can use the bathroom first," he motioned for her to go ahead of him.

Liliana nodded in his direction and walked through his bedroom to the small bathroom. Closing the door behind her, she stared at herself in the mirror.

Her hair was frizzy and sticking up in all directions, giving her a wild, crazed look and smoke smudged her face. She was going to need much more than Dante's powder to make herself presentable for dinner.

A hot wave of embarrassment washed over her. How was it

that the warlock's curls were still in place and hers were a mess? Pushing the thoughts aside, she turned the water on and grabbed a cloth from the hanger.

Outside the door, she could hear music playing and Dante's deep voice humming along. It was one of the love ballads he always played.

The vision of him dancing with Giordana at Alessia's wedding filled her mind. His movements were graceful and well-practiced. His smile charming. Realizing she was squeezing the cloth tightly in her fist, she loosened her grip and used it to wipe her face and hands.

After fixing her hair and powdering her dress, she opened the door to let Dante have the bathroom. He stepped past her, body nearly brushing hers.

His dark eyes leapt to hers. "I'll be out in a moment."

Skin prickling at his nearness, she nodded and moved away from him. He disappeared into the bathroom, shutting the door.

Liliana looked around his bedroom. Her gaze snagged on the giant bed in the middle. Images of him shirtless filled her mind, making her pulse race. She shook the thoughts away and turned to look at the dresser table on the opposite side. How was she going to spend another night with the warlock? How much longer would his friend's love spell last? Surely, it had to fade soon.

Dante hummed from the bathroom, the off-key sound making her smile.

No. She couldn't let herself fall for him. Once the spell was broken, they'd go back to being rivals.

* * *

"You're late!" Serafina called from the path behind them.

Liliana scoffed. "So are all of you."

Dante, who'd brought the horse and cart to a stop inside the gate, offered Liliana a hand down from the cart.

Wary of the spell, Liliana pretended not to notice his hand and jumped to the ground on her own. The less she touched him, the better.

They turned to the arriving party walking through the open gate.

"Have Alessia and Massimo already arrived?" Fiorella asked as she greeted them.

"We just arrived. I don't know if they're here or not," Liliana answered.

Serafina made a face. "I hope Angelo isn't coming this time."

"Why wouldn't he? He's Salvatore's brother," Liliana said with a snort.

Her sister turned a fierce glare on her. "So? That doesn't mean they have to invite him for everything."

Pamina motioned for Serafina to stop talking. "Don't be rude, Fina. Angelo has always been kind to our family."

Serafina gaped at her. "Are you forgetting the time he called me freckled face? Or played that nasty trick on our poor horse?"

Liliana shook her head. "You do have freckles and wasn't that prank to get you back for..." noticing Dante's curious stare, she let her words trail off.

"Sending snakes up his trousers?" Fiorella asked with a wide grin.

Dante made a choking sound, trying to hide his amusement. Liliana glanced at her mother, who looked oblivious to the conversation. Instead, she was studying Dante a little too much. At Liliana's stare, her mother's gaze darted to her, a questioning look in her brown eyes.

The others started walking up the stone path to the villa. Mama touched Liliana's arm and motioned for her to walk with her. Dante threw her a 'are you alright?' look. At Liana's nod, he followed the others.

"What is it? Have you found a way to break the spell?" Liliana asked, lowering her voice.

Mama frowned. "I'm sure the spell will fade in time, *amore*. Don't worry."

"I don't have time, Mama. I want this to be over with. Now."

A knowing look crossed her mother's face, but she said nothing. Lifting the hem of her dress, she walked beside Liliana and stared straight ahead.

"Do you remember my vision? The child?" Mama asked, breaking the silence.

Liliana sucked in a breath and looked around to make sure no one was listening. They were alone on the path. Shoulders relaxing, she turned to her mother with a frown. "I remember. What about it?"

"Well, I thought at first it was yours, but now... I'm not so sure."

"What do you mean you're not sure? Why did you think it was mine to begin with anyway?"

Mama shrugged. "She had large, brown eyes and dark curls, but her complexion was darker than yours. More like..." she nodded in the direction the others had gone.

Liliana's heart leapt into her throat. "You think you saw Dante's child?"

She didn't know why that thought both excited and scared her at the same time.

"Visions are tricky, *amore*. But I do get the feeling that this child... while it may be his, it's not... it's not yours," Mama said, an apologetic look on her face.

Liliana turned away with a scoff. "Of course, it's not! I never thought it was."

But she had. And when her mother had mentioned the child could be Dante's, there'd been a tiny part of her that had thought... wanted to believe that it could be her future too.

She shook her head. It was just the spell. She didn't really want to have a child with the warlock.

"Are you alright, Liliana?" Mama's voice snapped her back to the present.

"Of course. We should get inside for dinner," she said, walking quicker to catch up with the others.

"Liliana?" Mama asked, reaching a hand out to her.

"I'm fine," Liliana snapped, not slowing.

The chilly evening air swirled around them, cooling Liliana's heated skin. So, her mother had seen the future, but it was Dante's future. Not hers. Dante was going to have a child with someone else. What did that matter to her? Once the spell was broken, they'd go back to how they'd been before and that was just fine with her.

"Good evening!" Salvatore greeted them at the door.

"Signore," Adriano, his faun husband, nodded politely at them.

They returned his greeting and made their way into the front foyer where the others waited. Liliana avoided Dante's gaze and joined her sisters, forcing a smile on her face. As much as she wanted to deny it, her mother's revelation had shaken her.

She couldn't stop thinking about it.

"Will anyone else be joining us, Signore?" Serafina asked, as Salvatore led them through to the sitting room.

He glanced over his shoulder at her and shook his head. "Just us boring men tonight, I'm afraid, signorina. I'll give Angelo your regards next I seem him though."

Serafina flushed. "No. That's not—"

Salvatore turned away with a smirk. Fiorella giggled behind her hand, darting out of Serafina's reach.

"Everything alright?" Dante asked, sidling up to Liliana as they entered the parlor room.

"Of course. Why wouldn't it be?" She answered without looking at him.

He glanced at her mother and back to her. "You look upset."

Irritation filled her. How was it that he could read her so easily? What did he care anyway?

"I'm fine," she said, chin lifted.

Dante snorted. "Usually when a woman says she's fine—"

"Oh, and you're an expert on women, are you?" her voice rose above the chatter.

Everyone glanced at them. The fire in the fireplace crackled, the sound loud in the silence. Liliana's face flamed. The last thing she wanted was to have everyone think she was falling for the warlock. Just like all the other women.

A knock sounded from the front door, saving Liliana from the embarrassment.

Salvatore excused himself to see to their new arrivals, while Adriano struck up a conversation with Mama and Pamina. Serafina and Fiorella sank down on one of the sofas and whispered to each other, leaving Liliana alone with Dante and his imploring eyes.

Much to Liliana's relief, Salvatore reentered the room with Alessia and Massimo.

Massimo's pointed ears reddened at the tips. "Apologies, everyone. I lost track of time."

Alessia gave him an affectionate smile. "He's been buried with work, getting everything ready for the masquerade."

Massimo met her gaze. "You've done most of the work, *amore*. It's going to be beautiful."

A tightness filled Liliana's chest as she watched their loving exchange. She didn't listen as everyone started talking about the masquerade.

Alessia's gaze met hers. She walked over to Liliana and gave her a tight hug.

"It should be to Delle Rose by the end of the week," Alessia said softly.

"The letter?" she added at Liliana's blank stare.

"Yes. Thank you," Liliana said with a nod.

A worried look on her face, Alessia motioned for Liliana to follow her to the stone fireplace. Heat from the fire warmed Liliana all the way through. The smell of sweet wine and lasagna enveloped the room.

"I'm sorry I haven't checked in sooner. I was busy making the final preparations for the masquerade in town. Serafina told us the brea... it didn't work?" Alessia asked, lowering her voice.

Liliana glanced around to make sure no one was listening. "Only enough to give me time to clean myself up. We can only be apart for half an hour before the pain starts."

Alessia bit her lip. "What are you going to do about tonight? You two should come and stay with us. We have plenty of room,"

"We're going to try another breaking spell tonight. See if we can at least lengthen the time we can be apart. Fiorella brought us more lilies to use."

"Can't you move his cauldron?"

Liliana shook her head. "Not without using a lot of magic. It's fine. I'll be fine."

"How was it? Did he...?" her sister asked, a curious look on her face.

Liliana glanced at the handsome warlock. His dark eyes snapped to hers, a warm smile spreading on his lips. Her heart flip-flopped.

She shook her head and turned back to her sister. "It was fine. Thankfully, it doesn't seem to be affecting us that much."

Alessia's eyebrow arched in disbelief.

"Dinner is ready! Everyone to the dining room, please," Salvatore's rich voice interrupted them.

Giving her sister a reassuring smile, Liliana turned to follow the others. Dante joined her, offering his arm. With everyone's eyes on them, she couldn't refuse him. She placed her hand in his arm and braced herself. His warmth enveloped her, and his musky smell made her lightheaded.

"Are you alright?" he asked softly.

"Yes. Will you stop asking me that?" She replied, giving him a warning look.

"Will you stop avoiding me?"

She glanced at his face. "I'm not avoiding you. Let's just get through this night without making as scene, shall we?"

Before he could respond, she let go of his arm and took the seat Salvatore pulled out for her. Dante took the chair directly across from her.

Everyone else sat down around the table, the chatter filling the silence. Large platters of various vegetables and a giant basket of bread sat center of the table. The Rossi's cook came out with a platter of lasagna to serve them.

Holding a glass of wine aloft, Salvatore turned to Dante. "So, have you talked to Signor Marcello since you've met him?"

Dante took a sip of his wine and set it down. "Actually, yes. He stopped in this morning. Friendly fellow, isn't he?"

Salvatore chortled. "What did he want now?"

Dante darted a look at Liliana. "Well, he didn't drop in to congratulate me on my shop's opening."

"I imagine not. Was he furious? What did he say?" Salvatore asked, eyes gleaming.

Adriano patted him on the shoulder affectionately. "You'll

have to forgive my husband, Signore. He has quite the penchant for gossip."

Salvatore waved his words away and turned back to Dante. "That man is insufferable. Did you know that he's been all over town, spreading rumors that you two are in cahoots to poison everyone at the masquerade?"

"What?" Liliana asked, heatedly.

Dante chuckled. "Is he now?"

"Oh! Massimo, you must speak to him. What if he stirs everyone up? No one will want to come to the masquerade," Alessa said, giving her husband a worried look.

"Of course, *amore*. I'll speak to him first thing in the morning. This is unacceptable," the fae answered with a frown.

Liliana snorted. "He's ruining my reputation —again— and you're worried about the masquerade?"

"And what about mine as well?" Dante spoke up.

Alessia gave Liliana an apologetic look. "Well, of course, I'm upset about that too, Liliana. That man has been a thorn in your side since... forever, but how are we supposed to host the masquerade if he has everyone believing we mean to poison them?"

Serafina snorted. "If they truly believe that, then they are even stupider than they look."

"Fina," Pamina admonished her with a shake of her head.

"It's Hallow's Eve. It has everyone on edge. I'm sure a word from their count will put everyone's minds at ease," Mama spoke up. She gave Massimo a nod of approval.

The fae, who didn't like crowds or giving speeches, gave Alessia a worried look. She squeezed his hand in encouragement.

"Did you tell them about your first encounter with the man?" Salvatore asked Dante.

At the warlock's shake of the head, Salvatore turned to

regale everyone with the tale. Liliana tried to listen as the conversation flowed around her, but her mother's words echoed in her mind.

She needed to break the spell and cut off ties with the warlock before she did anything stupid. The words of the spell came to her. *Find your true match.* She swallowed the lump in her throat. She wasn't Dante's true match. Once the spell was broken, he would move on and so would she.

Chapter 14

Lover's Quarrel

Dante

The conversation around the table dragged on long into the night. As hospitable as the hosts were and as delicious as the food was, Dante was ready to leave. He longed to return to his shop and have alone time with Liliana. He couldn't help but feel as if something had changed between him and the beautiful witch.

She'd seemed fine before. They'd been working together nicely all day. For the most part, at least. It had to be something her mother had said to her. But what could it be?

"Did they tell you about the last dinner we had? At the Count's villa?" Salvatore's booming voice interrupted Dante's thoughts.

He glanced at the others and frowned. "No, I don't believe so."

"It was before you arrived," Massimo explained from the other end of the table.

"Yes. For Liliana's birthday," Alessia added, nodding in the direction of her sister.

Dante turned to the quiet witch, who was studiously ignoring him.

As if the lasagna could possibly be that entertaining.

Salvatore continued, his voice echoing in the dining room. Dante caught bits and pieces of the story. Something about Serafina, Massimo's cat, and Salvatore's younger brother who had apparently needed a change of pants by the end of the dinner.

The story ended in chorus of chuckles and head shakes.

"It was your birthday?" Dante asked, turning to Liliana.

Her dark eyebrow arched. "That's what you took out of all that?"

Everyone's heads swiveled in their direction, their eyes wide with curiosity and amusement. Massimo and Alessia shared a wary look, but Dante was too preoccupied with what he'd just learned to pay them any attention.

"Why didn't you tell me your birthday had passed?"

She shrugged off his question. "Because it isn't that important."

Dante frowned. "Well, I disagree. I think every birthday is important and should be celebrated."

Liliana set down her fork, giving him her full attention. "Pamina made me cannoli. I got presents from my family. It was just what I wanted. I don't need some big, fancy party."

"Was there dancing at least?" Dante asked, unable to help himself.

Irritation flashed on Liliana's face. "I don't like dancing."

Salvatore coughed, shifting uncomfortably. He glanced at his husband, with a questioning look as if to ask if he should interject or let the conversation play out. Adriano gave him an unhelpful shrug.

Dante leaned back in his chair and regarded Liliana with a

raised brow. "Really? You don't like dancing? You seemed to be enjoying it at your sister's wedding if I recall."

"Funny that you can recall anything with all the wine you guzzled," Liliana answered with an innocent look.

"Liliana," Alessia spoke up, face flushing with embarrassment.

Dante felt his lips tug into an amused smile. At least she was talking to him now and not ignoring him. He'd never met anyone who could verbally spar with him so, matching him at every turn. His gaze dipped to Liliana's pursed lips. She did not look amused.

The clink of silverware and glasses filled the awkward silence. Much to everyone's relief, their cook chose that moment to enter with a tray of decadent looking desserts.

"Oh, these look amazing," Pamina gushed, swiping two custard tarts for herself.

The older woman smiled. "Thank you, Signora, but I'm afraid I can't take the credit. I bought these from Signor Covelli's bakery in town."

Murmurs of approval rippled through the group as caffé and dessert were served. Dante watched as Liliana sipped from her porcelain cup. Her eyes were downcast, long, dark lashes batting slowly.

She wouldn't even look at him now?

Dante tried to recall their earlier conversation to see if he'd said something to offend her, but he couldn't think of anything.

Turning his attention back to his plate, he pushed away the disappointment. It was probably for the best anyway. Once the spell faded, he'd be free of her and she of him.

* * *

The drive back down the mountain and to the shop was tense and quiet. Still unsure of what he'd said or done, Dante focused on the road, humming a ballad.

"You do know that you're off-tune, don't you?" Liliana's question made him glance over.

He smirked. "Oh, are you talking to me now?"

She looked away, pulling her shawl tighter around herself. Dante fought the urge to roll his eyes. There wasn't much room on the bench, but the stubborn witch seemed determined to sit as far away from him as possible. As if his mere touch repulsed her.

Despite their distance, Dante's skin still prickled at her presence. Her lavender soap drifted with the cool night breeze, teasing him. The sky was beginning to darken above them.

"Ah. Back to the silence. Well, tonight should be fun," Dante muttered, his breath puffing out.

The wagon wheels crunched on the fallen leaves and dirt, filling the silence. Liliana shot him a glare before folding her arms across herself and turning to stare at the road ahead.

"I just hope no one is out to see us together like this," she finally spoke, brow furrowed.

Irritation filled Dante at her words.

"Yes, because being seen with me would be the absolute worst."

"They would get the wrong idea," she answered, not meeting his eyes.

"And what idea is that?" he pressed, hoping to needle her. See if she would admit her attraction. Maybe even lower her defenses for a little bit.

"That... we care for each other."

Dante's chest tightened. "And we don't?"

A laugh escaped her, sounding harsh. "Of course not. We

122

were forced into this by your friend. I'll be happy when things go back to normal."

Forced.

Dante grew quiet, her words ringing in his ears. Whatever progress he'd thought they'd been making, he'd been wrong. She still hated him just as much as ever.

"I promise you, as soon as this spell is broken, we'll never have to work together again," she added softly.

"Is it that awful working with me? I thought we made a good team," Dante said with a frown.

Liliana stiffened beside him. "Your skills are... adequate, but I prefer to work on my own."

He snorted, drawing her attention. Of course, she did. Little miss perfect. How could he ever think he'd be good enough for her?

She glared at him. "I don't know why that's so amusing."

"Really? You're so set on acting like you don't need anyone. Like—"

"I don't need anyone. Least of all you."

Her words felt like a slap to the face.

"Yes, because I'm so repulsive to you. Funny that you find me so arrogant when you're the one with the upturned nose."

Liliana huffed. "I don't find you repulsive. It's just... you take everything so lightly. Does nothing matter to you?"

"My magic matters," Dante said firmly, hands tightening on the reins.

The heavy clomp of the horse echoed in the quiet.

"Is that all?" she asked, voice so soft he almost didn't hear it.

"There's nothing more important to me than my magic. It's all I have. It's all I want," he answered with a shrug.

His mentor's words replayed in his mind. *Magic isn't everything. You're not as happy with being alone as you pretend to be.*

Maybe he wasn't, but he would have to learn to be. The

alternative—trying to love someone who already saw him as a failure—would only lead to heartache for both of them.

Dante looked over to the brooding witch. Her expression was hard and unreadable. Each time he thought she was lowering her defenses, she would push him away once more.

"If I did or said something, recently that is, to upset you, I'm sorry,"

Liliana didn't meet his gaze. "You haven't."

Dante stopped the cart and turned his attention to her. "Is it just me or do you insist on shutting everyone out?"

Her eyes snapped to his. The shattered look she gave him cut through him like a knife. Her sharpness, he was beginning to realize, was armor. A shield to protect herself.

"You've been hurt before," he said, unable to hide his realization.

She looked away. "What do you care?"

Dante frowned. "You don't have to tell me if you don't want to, but whoever it was, whatever happened... I'm sorry."

The wounded expression on her face twisted his heart. He'd never seen her so vulnerable before.

"It was nothing. Just a silly girlhood crush. I thought... I was stupid. He only wanted one thing and once he got it... he went back to seeing me as just a witch. Just like everyone else."

Her confession made Dante's blood boil. He couldn't stand the thought of her going through that.

"Bastard. I hope you put a hex on him," Dante said, continuing the drive.

Liliana smirked. "A rash. In the most inconvenient of places. And a silencing spell so he couldn't talk about... any of it."

"Hmm. That doesn't seem like enough. You should have had Serafina send snakes up *his* trousers," Dante said with a grunt.

She looked at him. "You're the only one besides Alessia who knows about this."

Dante glanced over at her, eyebrow arched. She was telling him her darkest secret? He could hardly believe it. Though it touched him, he couldn't but feel the seriousness of it.

What if he messed up this new and fragile bond? Let her down?

You are a disappointment. The words of his father echoed from the past.

They drove the rest of the way in silence, lost in their own thoughts. The sun had nearly set completely by the time Dante had the wagon and horse stabled.

He glanced around at the empty street and smiled at the sight before him. The streetlamps were lit, their golden glow lighting up the cobblestones. Garlands of red, brown, and yellow leaves were strung from post to post and over shop windows. Even the homes were decorated with autumn wreathes and banners.

A loud shriek pulled him out of his thoughts. He turned to see Ometta flying out the back door as Liliana opened it.

Pulling his scarf tighter around his neck, he closed the stable doors and went to join her.

"I hope it's okay that I let her out. She was by the door," Liliana said, eyes meeting his.

Dante nodded in response and followed her back inside. His room glowed with candlelight. The waxy smell filled the room along with the crisp autumn air. Dante shivered.

He would need a small heater for his room before the winter. It would be much too cold for them. For him. The realization that soon, once they were free, Liliana would return to her family struck him. No more waking up to her handing him his caffé. No more working side by side.

Dante shook the thoughts away. No more sleepless nights. No more bickering.

"Aren't you going to leave the door open for Ometta?" Liliana's question drew him back to the present.

"Oh, I spelled the door. From now on, it will open for her when she's ready. I figured you were right that we shouldn't leave it open all night."

A look of surprise flashed across her face.

She turned away with a nod and pulled a giant woolen night dress over her day dress. Dante bit back a smile.

"We could do a warming spell, you know. You don't have to sleep in all those... layers."

Liliana turned to him with a frown. "I'm fine."

Giving up, Dante walked past her and looked down at the cot in the corner. He stifled a groan.

"I suppose it's back to the cot for me?" he asked, eyes darting to Liliana.

She glanced over at him from underneath the covers. "We could... share the bed?"

Her suggestion made him nearly choke. "Are you sure?"

Liliana frowned. "Do you promise to keep your hands and all other... body parts to yourself?"

Dante couldn't hide his grin. "I promise. Can you promise?"

Ignoring his teasing, the witch moved over and turned away from him. Heart hammering against his ribcage, Dante joined her, pulling the heavy quilt up to his chest. Warmth radiated from her along with the strong smell of her soap.

He realized, too late, how hard it would be to keep his promise. Everything inside him screamed to edge closer to her. To touch her dark curls. Kiss her full lips.

Turning to his side, he bit back a groan. How was he supposed to sleep now? Silence surrounded them.

"Hopefully, we'll receive a reply to our letter before the

masquerade. Before Hallow's Eve. The last thing we want is for this to become permanent," Dante said, interrupting the quiet.

Liliana turned around to face him. "Permanent?"

Dante met her horrified look. "Well, there's no telling what the magic will do on Hallow's Eve. Spells can become... unpredictable."

"If we don't receive a reply from your mentor, then I'll go and find her myself. Get her to put an end to this nonsense at once."

Too tired to respond, Dante turned back over and stared at the wall. The candles cast shadows along it, shapes moving in the flickering light.

"Goodnight," Liliana said softly.

"Night," Dante returned, refusing to turn and look at her.

He didn't want to be reminded of what he'd be losing once the spell was broken. What he'd spoken to her was true. Spells could be altered on Hallow's Eve. What if their bond did become permanent on Hallow's Eve? Dante didn't know which was worse.

He had grown rather fond of Liliana and would miss their time together but being free of her and the expectations... he'd be free to follow his own path once more. That would be better for everyone.

Chapter 15

Final Preparations

Liliana

Something stirred beneath Liliana. Something warm and solid. A hand brushed her hair from her face. She woke with a start. Her eyes met Dante's.

She had fallen asleep, nestled against his broad chest.

He gave her an exasperated smile. "Sorry to wake you, but I really need the bathroom."

Face reddening, she moved away, heat spreading through her. She was too warm under all her layers now. Dante slid off the bed and walked to the bathroom, glancing back at her with a strange look. Did he think she had purposefully spread herself across him?

Fighting back a groan, she stood up and pulled off the heavy robe. Dante's deep voice echoed from the bathroom. Liliana knew all his favorite ballads by heart now.

The memories of the night before flooded her as she got ready. Her mother's words. The dinner. The ride back to town. Why had she told him her secret?

It had to be the spell at work, making her lower her

defenses. Liliana shook her head. She had to be stronger. She couldn't let herself fall for Dante.

"Did you sleep well?" the warlock's voice startled her out of her thoughts.

Liliana turned to see him standing in the door of the bathroom, watching her. His heated gaze made her flush. He'd taken off his night shirt and stood in his loose trousers, chest on full display.

"Ahem. My eyes are up here," he said with amusement.

Liliana's gaze snapped to his. A wicked grin spread on his face. He took a step toward her.

"I'm going to start the fire. We need to finish the barrier spells today," Liliana said, turning on her heel.

She could still feel his stare as she left. The attraction between them was impossible to ignore. It was dangerous. Dante had already proven he wasn't the type to stick around long.

My magic is all I need. All I want.

She'd be a fool to give in. She couldn't go through another heartbreak. The first time had nearly destroyed her.

Pushing away the dark memories, Liliana hurried to the little kitchen. The chill of the autumn air filled the room, making her shiver.

Dante, now dressed, joined her, and headed straight for the cupboard to pull out two mugs. "Caffè? How do you take it?"

Liliana turned to look at him.

He smiled at her. "Let me guess. Black?"

"Just sugar," she said, turning back to the hearth.

Dante shrugged. "I'll get it right eventually."

The sound of the liquid pouring into the cups filled the

silence along with the crackle of fire. Liliana lifted her chapped hands to the growing flames.

"Here you are," Dante said, walking over to her and handing her the steaming mug.

Liliana took it with grateful nod.

After a slow sip from his own cup, Dante gave her a lazy smile. "Look at us. Practically best friends now, right?"

Her eyebrow arched at him. "Right. Two birds of a feather."

"I can't tell if you're being sarcastic or not," Dante said between sips.

"Are you going to hurry and finish your caffé so you can help me?"

Dante set his mug down on the little table and walked back over to the cauldron. He stood with his hands on his hips and peered into the bubbling mixture.

"As much as I love brewing. One never gets used to the smell." He made a face.

"What's on the agenda for today, darling?" he asked.

Liliana's heart skipped at the address. Ignoring the ache she felt, she pointed at the crate of talismans. "Massimo is holding a meeting in the plaza today and will have Patrizio Foncello hand out the talismans. We'll finish the barrier spells while they do that."

"Sounds simple enough. Before I forget, we should do a locating spell as well. Make sure there are no other portals or gates nearby," Dante said with a serious look.

"We'll need a map for that. Patrizio Foncello has the only map of Zamerra and I'm not sure he'll be willing to give it to us for a spell."

Dante's eyes widened in surprise. "No one else owns a map?"

Liliana shrugged. "Not of Zamerra. Everyone here already knows where everything is."

"Good thing I brought mine then," Dante said, walking over to the kitchen counter. He pulled out a stack of parchment papers from the cupboard and smiled at Liliana.

Liliana watched as he spread them out on the little table with care. Most of the maps were marked with circles and inscriptions along the edge.

She met Dante's eyes. "You've been to all these places?"

He shrugged. "I get restless."

A strange ache filled her at his words. Was Zamerra just one stop to the next place for him? Suddenly the thought of him leaving made her sad. But of course, he would leave. There was nothing keeping him there.

She took a sip of her caffé and swallowed the lump in her throat. "We should get started then."

At his nod, she set down her mug and started preparing the spell.

* * *

"This is the last of it. Everything is all set for Hallow's Eve after this," Liliana said, rubbing her forehead.

Dante's eyes traveled across her face. He smiled.

"What?" she asked him.

"You're breath-taking. Smudges and all," he said, picking up a wet rag.

Liliana sucked in a breath as he gently wiped her cheek and chin with the warm cloth. His gaze dropped to her lips, making her face heat. His woodsy scent filled her lungs as he stood near her. Dark eyes bore into hers.

Taking the rag from him, Liliana fought the urge to shudder. Did he feel the pull too? Did he feel the same rush of heat and desire?

Liliana turned away and dropped the rag into the sink. Her

potion-stained fingers had left dark marks on it. She stared at the spots, a wave of emotion rising inside of her.

The more time she spent with Dante, the stronger the power of the spell grew. Like the rag, he'd left a permanent mark on her. One, she was beginning to fear, she would never recover from. What happened when the spell broke?

"We have some time before Massimo calls the meeting. Shall we go for lunch? There's nothing left to eat here," Dante's voice startled her.

Liliana washed her hands and glanced back at him. He was gathering up the maps from the table. She reached for the hanging towel to dry her hands at the same time as he opened the cupboard above it.

His body stood so close to hers, his warmth enveloped her. The memory of his solid chest beneath her made her skin prickle.

She turned around to face him, their faces mere inches apart. Liliana could smell the caffè on his breath.

His dark eyes found hers. "Are you okay? Your face looks flushed."

Before Liliana could respond, a loud knock came from the front of the shop. Dante frowned and moved away. Cool air swirled in the space he'd left. Liliana watched him leave the kitchen, her heart still racing.

She shut her eyes and tried to calm herself. The pull was getting too strong. Too hard to ignore. Though if she were being honest, the attraction had been there before. Dante's words from the wedding rang in her ears.

I want to touch you. Taste you.

A snap from the fire brought her back to the present. What they had now was temporary. Liliana smiled sadly at the silver cauldron. She would miss using it. It brewed the ingredients for spells much quicker than her old iron one.

"I'm afraid I'm still not quite ready to open the shop. However, it will be open after Hallow's Eve," Dante's deep voice came from the front.

"Oh, but I'm sure you could make an exception. For me?" came the unmistakable sugary voice of Giordana.

Liliana scowled at her flirtatious tone. Before she realized what she was doing, she was out the door and marching up to Dante's side.

She opened the door wider to glare at her. "You heard him, Giordana. We're closed. Come back after Hallow's Eve," Liliana said, unable to hide the iciness in her words.

Giordana's eyes widened in shock. She glanced from Liliana to Dante. "So, it's true then? Signor Marcello said you two had formed some kind of... partnership."

Her lips pursed as if she'd eaten something sour.

Liliana gave her a brilliant smile. "I didn't take you for one who listened to gossip."

The young woman glared. "Well, I didn't take you for a such a light-skirt, Liliana."

Before Liliana could respond, Dante waved a hand between them.

He frowned at Giordana. "I assure you, Signorina, our business is strictly professional."

Liliana grabbed his hand and pulled it out of the doorway. "Our business is none of *your* business. Good day, Giordana."

With that, she shut the door and threw up a locking spell. A gasp of outrage came from the other side, making Liliana smile.

Dante's eyebrow arched at her. "Well."

He blinked at her, at a loss for words. Liliana shrugged and walked back to the kitchen to finish cleaning. Dante followed behind her, his presence making her body thrum with awareness.

"We can clean the rest later. Let's go for lunch," Dante said as he walked over to her.

Liliana bit her lip. Working in the apothecary with the handsome warlock was one thing, but she knew the minute they stepped out together, everyone would start talking about them. Giordana had probably already started spreading rumors.

Nobody knew about her past mistakes, but given Dante's reputation, there would be assumptions made if they saw her with him out at one of the restaurants.

Dante grunted, drawing her attention.

"It's just lunch, Liliana. A business lunch. No one will think anything more of it," he said with a shrug.

The casualness in his tone stung. Though she knew she had no right to get upset after she'd made it plainly clear to him that she didn't want to be spotted with him. Once the spell faded or was broken, they'd go back to as they were before.

Liliana squared her shoulders back and gave him a nod. "Where do you want to eat? There are only three options in Zamerra."

He smiled, making her stomach flutter. "Your choice. Before we get ready, I'll cover the cauldron. Just in case."

Liliana watched as he walked over and slid the metal lid over the cauldron.

She sighed. "I'm going to miss your cauldron. When the spell fades, I mean. Or if we are finally able to break it."

He turned back to her and winked. "You can always come over and use it. Anytime you want. Anything of mine, you'd like."

A scoff escaped Liliana. "Even Ometta?"

Dante scratched his clean-shaven chin and gave her a slight nod. "You've never used a familiar before?"

"Not until now. I'm afraid my magic isn't powerful enough

to warrant one." Liliana couldn't hide the wistfulness in her voice.

Dante gave her a meaningful look. "Or maybe the time hasn't come yet."

Liliana shook her head. "I'm twenty and four. I think my time has come and passed." She shrugged. "I've accepted that. I'll never be more than just a simple potion witch."

He frowned. "You are much more than that."

Silence stretched between them. His words rang in her ears, warming her through. As silly as it was, his compliment touched her. No one else understood her magic like he did.

"Thank you," she finally spoke. "You are too," she added quickly, shifting awkwardly to her other foot.

Dante grinned. "Not mediocre?"

"Not mediocre," she agreed, turning away before he could see her blush.

"I think that's the nicest compliment you've given me," Dante continued, a lightness in his voice.

As much as Liliana hated to admit it, his sunniness was starting to thaw her icy heart. Their time together had revealed him to be much more than the flirtatious warlock she believed him to be.

Would she still feel the same when the spell was broken?

Dismissing those worrisome thoughts, Liliana walked away to freshen up in the bathroom. Once they were both ready, Dante led her out of the shop.

The outside air was so cold it nearly stole Liliana's breath. She pulled her shawl tighter to ward off the chill.

Dante gave her a side-eyed glance. "I could enchant that for you, if you wish. Make it warmer."

He held up the end of his woolen red scarf as an example. Liliana shook her head and kept walking.

"Magic shouldn't be used so frivolously," she said, sounding just like her mother.

It was one of the few things they agreed on.

Dante shrugged and threw the scarf back with a grin. His wide smile made Liliana's heart flutter. There was no denying his appeal. They had barely started walking and already heads were turning to them. To Dante.

Liliana lifted her chin, refusing to show a reaction to their disapproving stares and whispers. She walked along the cobblestones, matching the warlock's long strides. Feeling his eyes on her, she turned her head slightly toward him.

For once, he wasn't smiling. Instead, he watched her. The intensity of his gaze nearly made her stumble. There was something written in his dark eyes that made a jolt of awareness run through her.

He was looking at her as if he was seeing her for the first time. Face growing warm, Liliana tore her eyes away and stared at their path ahead.

Around them, the townsfolk were busy preparing for the masquerade. Hand-painted signs and wreaths went up. Banners were spread from roof to roof. Voices rang through the streets and the chimney smoke from the shops and homes filled the crisp autumn air.

They made it to the little osteria on the corner where a line of people stood outside the open door. There were only three tables on the street and they were all full. The inside was probably fully occupied too.

Liliana turned to Dante. "Do you want to wait? Or we could walk down to the restaurant?"

Dante met her eyes and smiled. "I don't mind waiting with you."

A strange look crossed his face. For a moment he looked as if he wanted to say more but stopped himself.

"We don't have much time to wait. The count is coming to make his speech," an older woman's voice interrupted them.

She crossed her arms across her chest and gave her companion a pointed look.

The man just nodded and gave her a patient smile. "Yes, *amore*. We'll make it in time."

Liliana recognized them from previous sales. The Zappas. They'd been married for as long as Liliana could remember. A twinge of longing filled her as she watched them.

Your true match. The words from the love spell came to her unbidden.

She glanced up at Dante, chest tightening. Could he be her match? Could her mother be wrong about her vision?

Dante noticed her stare and gave her a questioning look.

Shaking away the thoughts, Liliana glanced away.

She couldn't let herself fall for him. She'd already made the mistake of believing in love before and look where that had gotten her. What she had with Dante was just temporary. It didn't mean anything.

The line moved up and Liliana took a step forward, sighing inwardly. The sooner they broke the spell, the better off they'd both be.

Chapter 16

The Masquerade

Liliana

"Is everything ready for Hallow's Eve tomorrow?" Pamina asked, handing Liliana a mug of caffé.

Liliana took it with a grateful smile and took a sip, letting the warm, smooth liquid slide down her throat.

She nodded. "As much as possible, yes."

"Are you alright?" Pamina asked, joining her at the kitchen table.

The smell of cinnamon and sugary pastries was so strong, it masked the dried garlic and herbs hanging from the rafter hooks behind them. Bruno sat on the table between them, nibbling on a tart.

"I'm fine," Liliana answered absentmindedly, staring at the roaring fire in the hearth. Wood splintered and cracked, the sound loud in the quiet.

It was a rare moment when the villa was that calm or when it was just the two of them. The others had gone to town to help Alessia and Massimo with the final decorations, and Dante was locking up his shop in preparation. He'd be back soon before their breaking spell wore off.

Pamina sighed, drawing Liliana's attention. She laid a gentle hand atop of Liliana's. "It's okay to admit to your true feelings, Liliana."

She cut Liliana's protest off with another pat. "You've been the happiest I've ever seen you. Shouldn't that count for something?"

Liliana shook her head. "It's not that simple. We're not... he's not... the committing type. He's told me as much. I'd be a fool to fall for him."

Pamina frowned. "He may not be ready to admit it yet, but I think you've changed him."

"People don't change, Pamina."

"That's not always true."

"It is. The only one you can count on in life is yourself."

"Well, that's a bleak way of looking at things. You can't really believe that, Liliana. I think sometimes you don't give people a chance. No one is perfect."

"Now you sound like Mama," Liliana said with a grunt.

She took a sip from her mug and studied her sister. At only twenty-one, her little sister was growing up. Funny how that happened right before her and yet somehow she had missed it.

"I just don't want you to make any decision you'll regret," Pamina said softly, her light brown eyes on Liliana's.

Too late for that.

Pamina didn't know her secret. The heartbreak she'd experienced long ago. Only Alessia and Dante knew her reason for being so guarded.

"I just want you to be happy, Liliana," Pamina said with a sigh.

Before Liliana could assure her she was happy with her choices, the yard cats and Gio started fussing, interrupting them. Liliana's skin hummed with awareness.

Dante was back.

Pamina rose to her feet and opened the back door to see who had come. Dante entered, bringing in the cold air with him.

His dark eyes leapt to Liliana, excitement showing on his face. "Everything is set. The masquerade is going to be marvelous. And who knows, maybe with luck, this last breaking spell will break the love spell. By tomorrow, we could be free!"

Liliana's heart dropped into her stomach. She forced a smile. Pamina was wrong. She hadn't changed Dante. He was still the same flighty warlock she knew him to be. Their time together hadn't meant anything. Not to him.

Finishing the rest of her caffé, she stood up and nodded at him. "Good. When will it be ready?"

He shrugged. "We have one more attempt before midnight on Hallow's Eve. Either the spell will be permanent then or it will fade forever."

Fade forever.

What if it became permanent? Would he resent being stuck with her for life? Liliana didn't want to let him go just yet, but she didn't want him to grow resentful of their connection either.

Pushing away the thoughts, she washed her mug in the sink and set it on the cloth to dry. "We should get back to town and do another check on the barriers."

Dante frowned. "We've done enough checks. We should relax and enjoy ourselves. Rest up for all the dancing tonight," he said with a wide grin.

Liliana scoffed. "I'm not dancing. You can dance all you want. I'm sure Giordana will be thrilled."

His smile faltered.

Pamina shook her head, giving Liliana a pointed look. There was a silent message there. One that Liliana had heard one too many times before. She was pushing Dante away.

She was good at pushing people away. If she built a strong

enough wall around herself then she wouldn't be disappointed when things inevitability fell apart.

Despite what her sister believed, there was no happy ending in store for her and Dante. At least not one that included them together.

* * *

The town plaza was alive with music and dancing. Feathers, fur, and silk from the costumes clashed together, looking like something from a bizarre dream. Music filled the square, floating on the cold breeze. Fires were lit in the chimeneas and torches the townsfolk had placed around. Flames licked the night sky, the wood crackling and popping along with the musicians' notes.

"Ooh, let's dance!" Fiorella said, pulling Serafina by the arm. They'd chosen cat masks that matched their brown and red velvet dresses.

Mama nodded at them and waved them away. Pamina smiled, her lips and eyes the only thing visible in her delicate, feathery mask. She'd gone as a dove.

"I'm going to take this tray over to the banquet table," She shouted over the noise.

Mama followed, dressed as a fox, leaving Liliana alone in the crowd.

Her throat turned dry as she looked around at the masked faces. None of them were Dante. Where was he? He'd chosen to stay in town while she got ready with her sisters. A pressing need welled up inside of her.

Just the effects of the spell.

It would go away once they'd broken it. A strange sorrow filled her at the thought. She snorted, shaking her head at her own foolishness. It wasn't as if she'd never see the warlock again. Zamerra was a small town after all.

As if on cue, her eyes snagged on a black-clad figure walking into her line of sight. She sucked in a breath.

Dante.

He was dressed in a silk black suit lined with silver. He turned his head toward her, his eyes looking darker as they peered out of a sharp-beaked silver mask. His short curls hung around his face. He looked every bit the powerful warlock that he was. Regal. Mysterious. Dangerous.

A thrill went up Liliana's spine as he walked toward her, his movements purposeful. The crowd stopped and parted for him. Eyes followed him, mouths turned up in appraising smiles and whispers followed. Voices called after him in greeting.

He didn't stop to answer. Holding her gaze, he walked toward her.

Stopping in front of her, Dante bowed and took her hand in his.

Warmth spread up her arms at his touch. They had an audience now, but surprisingly, she didn't care. Standing there with him felt right.

"A raven? My compliments to your Mama and sisters. They've worked their magic," he leaned in closer. "You're stunning." His voice was deep and gravelly.

Liliana flushed under his smoldering stare. "Thank you. Your suit is... every bit as fancy as I'd imagine it to be. It suits you."

Dante grinned. "I'm glad you like it. And to think I almost went as a peacock." He winked playfully at her behind his mask.

An inelegant snort escaped her.

"Shall we go find the others?"

Liliana let him lead her, her hand in his arm. Heat rippled

through her at the contact. They walked through the crowd in silence, a heavy tension filling the space between them.

Trying to clear her mind, Liliana glanced around at the decorations and smiled. Zamerra had been transformed into something magical and breathtaking. Silver and gold banners hung from roof to roof. Candles were lit in every windowsill. Everyone was out for the masquerade.

"It's a good thing our spells included fire containment. Imagine how quickly a fire would spread here," Dante said, breaking her out of her revelry.

He pointed out the fiery torches lining the buildings and the lit streetlamps.

At the end of the square, a spread fit for royalty had been set out. Table after table was covered with heaping dishes of pastas, soups, and an array of desserts. The savory scent mixed with sweet filled the air. The silver tablecloths sparkled in the candle and firelight like stars.

Liliana glanced at Dante.

He shrugged. "A little enchantment on the tablecloth. It needed something,"

"It's beautiful," she admitted, glancing around the plaza.

The water in the fountain also sparkled silver and gold. Another enchantment that had turned the ordinary into something from a fairy tale.

Liliana's chest tightened. Soon the fairy tale would end. The spell would be broken, and everything would be set back to the way it was before.

"May I have this dance?" Dante asked, soft voice interrupting her inner turmoil.

Liliana met his stare. There was a 'no' waiting on the tip of her tongue, but it wouldn't come. In spite of everything, she wanted to dance with him. She wanted this night to last. She wanted to live in the fairy tale for a little bit longer.

Her heart pounded as she nodded in response. "Just one," she said.

The brilliant smile Dante gave her made her stomach flip flop. He led her to the dance floor, his steps sure. Keenly aware of everyone's stares, Liliana held her head high and followed. They made their way past the crowd and to joined the others in the square.

Music blared from the musicians, the notes low and dreamy.

Dante pulled her tightly against him, their bodies pressed together. Liliana's pulse quickened. The heat from his body warmed her through. Awareness rippled across her skin.

Dark, brown eyes drilled into hers.

Did he feel it too? The spell pulling them together? Liliana had been so eager to break it and sever the ties that held them trapped, but now that the moment had come, she wasn't so sure she could.

Pamina's words echoed in the back of her mind.

You've changed him.

Was it true? She knew he had changed her. How she felt. What she wanted. Even with the spell gone, she couldn't erase what had happened between them. Much less what was happening now.

"If the spell doesn't break tonight, I guess we'll just have to accept the fact that we're destined to be together forever," Dante said with a teasing smile.

Before she could answer, the song stopped. They paused in the middle of the dance floor.

Dante's head lowered toward hers. A thrill ran up her spine.

"Do you know what I'm about to do?" he asked, voice hoarse.

Her gaze met his. The fire she saw burning in them made her flush. She could only nod.

Taking that as a yes, he closed the distance, claiming her lips with his. Several scandalized gasps echoed around them, but Liliana didn't care. She closed her eyes and tuned them out, lost completely in Dante's kiss.

She parted her lips, and he took her bottom lip between his teeth, giving a gentle tug. A wave of heat flooded her. She pressed in closer, just as hungry for his touch as he was for hers.

He tasted like sweet wine and his lips were like velvet. His fingers dug into her hips, his body so tight against hers that there was no denying his desire.

A moan escaped her.

With a small intake of breath, Dante pulled away, making her protest. His eyes were filled with fiery passion that seared into her skin. Breath ragged, Liliana tried to calm her racing heart. Her head spun as if she'd had too much wine.

The world around them blurred. Voices and music echoed them, sounding so far away. Liliana was vaguely aware of the bodies moving around them as the next song started.

Dante led her away from the crowd, his eyes peering out at her from his mask. She was filled with the sudden urge to pull it from his face, to see him in full.

Was his heart racing like hers was? Did his lips still feel hers on them?

Silence stretched between them. A raw ache spread in Liliana's chest. Why was he so quiet?

Dante stepped closer, his nearness making her heart race. She looked up to meet his gaze.

"I remember it. I remember everything I said to you at the wedding. I meant every word, too," his voice was low and gravelly.

Heat spread up Liliana's neck. She swallowed hard, suddenly feeling dizzy. He remembered?

"Oh," the word escaped her.

Dante's eyebrow arched. "Is that a good 'oh' or?"

Biting her lip, Liliana nodded slightly. "I... I don't know what to say."

He smiled. "Well, there's a first time for everything."

Taking her hands in his, he pulled her closer. "I've thought of that night for so long, you know. Of you. Even before the spell. There's no other woman I would have rather been stuck with like this."

Liliana felt her mouth drop in surprise.

"And if the spell is permanent after tonight, well, I think I can live with that," his gaze deepened.

"Can you?" he asked softly, eyes serious.

Before she could answer, a hand landed on her shoulder, interrupting their moment.

Liliana spun around to find Alessia. The worried look on her sister's face startled her.

"What is it? What's happened?" Liliana demanded.

Alessia shook her head, unable to speak. Liliana glanced at Dante in confusion. He frowned, sharing her puzzlement.

"It's Fiorella. She's missing. Along with Tito," Alessia finally answered with a grim face.

Chapter 17

Hallow's Eve

Dante

D ante sucked in a breath, trying to clear his head. His lips were tingling, and his skin felt flushed. Kissing Liliana had been everything he'd dreamed of and more.

He'd been so caught in the moment, it took him a minute to register what Alessia had said.

Liliana's fearful gaze snapped him out of the thoughts.

"We have to find her!" she called, turning away.

Dante hurried after her. *Find her.*

Fiorella was missing. So was her pet flower. Dante's stomach lurched. If the plant he'd given the young girl was responsible for something terrible he'd never forgive himself.

He glanced over at Liliana. She would never forgive him either. Tucking those thoughts away, he quickened his pace.

They made their way through the crowded plaza, calling out for Fiorella. Alessia stopped to ask the town leaders to make an announcement.

"In my shop! We can perform a locating spell," Dante said, waving for Liliana to follow him.

"Are you sure she didn't just go back to the villa?" Liliana asked her sister as they made their way down the street.

"Mama went to look. Pamina and Serafina went with her, and Massimo is checking the forest now. Oh, Liliana, where could she have gone?" Alessia's voice rose above the fading music, worry in her tone.

"We'll find her," Liliana said with a determined nod.

Dante exchanged a look with her. He didn't want to worry them, but the story Liliana had told him in the woods came to his mind.

Fiorella used to wander the woods, lured by whatever magic they held. Had the voices somehow become louder on Hallow's Eve, breaking through the barriers they'd set in place?

They made it to the apothecary, where he quickly unlocked the door to usher them all in. After a quick lighting spell, the shop was flooded with candlelight.

"Hurry," Liliana urged him, handing him one of the glass bottles containing the spell.

"Do you have anything of hers?" Dante asked, looking around at the others.

Alessia handed him the cat mask Fiorella had been wearing. Her eyes were watery as Liliana gave her a gentle squeeze on her shoulder.

Wasting no time, Dante uncorked the spell and directed it toward the mask, chanting the words aloud. Magic rippled in the air, leaving an acrid and smoky smell. Spell set, the mask glowed and floated in the air.

It would lead them to where Fiorella was.

"Thank you," Liliana said, dark eyes meeting his.

"I'll bring the wagon around," Dante said as the mask glided to the door and banged against the wood, trying to get out.

He ran out the back of the shop, stopping to let Ometta loose with special orders to help find Liliana's sister. Breathing in the chilly night air, he hurriedly hitched the wagon up to his horse and brough her around to the front.

"I'm ready," he announced, opening the front door of the shop.

The mask darted out, hovering above the wagon. Liliana and Alessia scrambled up the wooden bench with Dante's help. With a quick jerk of the reins, he followed as the mask started moving.

Liliana had removed her mask and a stricken look crossed her features. She grabbed his wrist as he led the horse down the street. "The Fairy gate. It was closed, wasn't? I closed it myself. It couldn't have opened, right?"

Dante shook his head. "I remember you performing the spell, but I didn't check the portal. We were... distracted."

Guilt filled him at the memory. He'd been too busy nursing his bruised ego and admiring Liliana's body to pay attention to the spell.

"We have to get to that gate," Liliana's urgent words snapped him to the present.

"What would happen if Fiorella activated it again? Would she get sucked in?" Alessia asked, voice wavering with worry.

"I... I don't know," Liliana answered.

She glanced at Dante. He shook his head slightly, wishing he could reassure her. There was no telling what Fiorella's magic would do. Hallow's Eve made things especially tricky.

Already he felt the crackling of magic in the air. Soon the spirits would pass over and through Zamerra. Everyone would be safe inside the plaza. He and Liliana had secured all the villas outside town too, but the magic of the forest was impossible to contain.

"She had her talisman, yes?" Dante asked them as he hurried the horse up the mountain.

Liliana looked to Alessia. Her sister only shook her head. "I don't know. She was wearing it earlier."

Fiorella's mask flew overhead, heading straight for the forest. Dante's heart sank. It was just as they'd suspected. Cursing himself for not arming himself with more spells, he pulled the wagon off the road and turned to help the women down from the it.

The forest was dark and deadly quiet.

"Massimo went to look for her in the forest near town. Should I go get him?" Alessia asked, eyes wide with worry.

Dante shook his head. "When he doesn't find her there, he'll come. We might need his fae blood to destroy the portal."

"Destroy it? But what about Fiorella?" The panic in Alessia's voice heightened.

Liliana squeezed her hand. "We're going to get her back."

She turned to Dante with a determined look. He nodded in agreement and led them toward the trees. They still had few hours before midnight. Anything could be reversed until the, couldn't it?

Choosing to hope for the best, he chanted a quick spell to light up the path before them. Leaves and debris crunched underfoot as they hurried through the forest.

"Fiorella!" Alessia called, her voice bouncing off the trees.

The night had transformed the woods into something ghastly. Long, thin branches spread out toward them like claws. The dark leaves above blended in with the night sky, looking like a giant mouth about to devour them.

Dante followed the sparkling mask, Liliana and Alessia hurrying beside him. Their fancy clothes rustled against the forest floor and overgrown shrubbery.

"There!" Liliana pointed ahead.

The Fairy gate glowed a bright white under the moonlight.

The mask stopped, hovering above the portal. Fiorella wasn't there.

Alessia gave a strangled cry.

Dante turned to Liliana. "We're too late. She's—"

"No! I'll go after her. I brought her back before. I can do it again," Liliana cut him off, marching toward the gate.

Dante blocked her path. "Hold on. The portals don't just open to anyone. You could be walking into your death, Liliana."

Another sob came from Alessia. Dante's heart twisted at the sound.

He met Liliana's fierce stare and knew there would be no stopping her.

"What about Massimo? He has fae blood. I can get him. He can help, can't he?" Alessia asked hopefully.

Dante turned to answer her, but a loud, shrill cry cut through the air.

"What was that?" Alessia asked, clinging to her sister's arm.

"Ometta. She found her," Dante said, hurrying toward the sound.

He didn't bother to explain, not wanting to waste any more time. Liliana and Alessia were right behind him. The path lit up before them as they ran, following the owl's call deeper into the woods.

The light from his spell was starting to fade. Dante cursed. He didn't want to waste his magic on another spell if he needed to cast defensive ones later, but they hadn't brought any lanterns or torches with them. A foolish mistake.

"What is that?" Alessia asked as a bright red glow lit up the forest.

Liliana gasped. "*Santo cielo!* Is that..."

"Tito?" Dante finished, staring in surprise at the giant plant.

Its massive red glowing head swiveled toward them, its sharp teeth opening and closing in quick succession.

"What happened to it?" Alessia asked, fear in her voice.

"Fiorella?" Liliana stepped forward.

Dante turned to see what she had seen. A small figure emerged from the trees.

Alessia gasped. "Ella?"

Dante shook his head. "No. That's Ometta."

The owl had transformed into her human form. Dark curls framed her child-like face and large, brown eyes stared blankly at them.

"Where is Fiorella?" Dante and Liliana asked Ometta in unison.

She pointed to Tito.

"What? Is she in there?" Liliana frowned, taking a cautious step toward the giant plant.

"Oh! What are we going to do?" Alessia cried.

"We'll destroy the plant. Get her back," Liliana said, hands lighting up with a spell.

Ometta tugged at Dante's sleeve. He turned back to her, opening his mind to her thoughts. In her child form, she couldn't talk. Pain speared through his temple as she quickly relayed the information to him.

"Wait!" He grabbed Liliana's arm before she could act.

"Tito isn't hurting her. It's keeping her safe," he explained what Ometta had told him.

Liliana frowned. "Keeping her safe? How?"

"From what?" Alessia asked.

Dante met Liliana's eyes. "A spirit. A powerful spirit has her. Tito is protecting her."

"A spirit? What does that mean?" Alessia turned to her sister.

Liliana stared at the plant. "But how? She has her talisman. It shouldn't have been able to—"

Before she could say more, Tito's head split wide open with

a sickening slicing sound. Dante jumped in front of Liliana and Alessia, hands lifted to shield them.

Fiorella emerged from the giant plant, her whole-body glowing a pale white. The talisman around her neck was cracked. Whether from her own doing or the spirit's, Dante didn't know.

As she floated toward them, eyes closed, Tito collapsed behind her, petals shaking loose. Its stalk and leaves shriveled and turned brown. The red glow from its head started to fade.

"Ella?" Liliana called, stepping around Dante.

"Careful," Dante warned, fingers curling and ready to cast.

He glanced at Ometta who had come to stand beside him. "Whatever possessed her is powerful enough to break free from Tito and Ometta's hold."

At this, Fiorella's eyes opened. Alessia gasped.

Instead of her usual green, they had turned bright red. Her face stretched into an odd smile, the air pulsating around her. Her long hair blew in all directions, as if moved by an imperceptible wind.

"Let her go!" Liliana demanded, eyes narrowed at her little sister.

She rolled her wrist, calling on her own magic.

Fiorella laughed. A strange, inhuman laugh. The guttural sound was frightening coming from her.

Dante stepped forward. "We need to get her back to the portal. Cast the spirit back to—"

Roots sprang up from the ground, striking at them. Dante threw up a shield just in time. The tree branches swayed, the noise of the rustling leaves growing deafening.

Whatever had a hold of Fiorella could draw from her magic, too. Surrounded by trees and plants, she had the upper hand.

Dante gave Ometta a silent look. She'd already depleted some of her magic by holding Fiorella back, but there was still enough power left in her child form before she'd be completely spent.

"Get her to the portal!" Dante called over the noise of the woods.

With a nod, Ometta cast an invisible net around Fiorella and started running toward the fairy gate.

Fiorella sputtered in rage, thrashing against the familiar's magic.

"Hurry, we don't have much time before she breaks out," Dante said, urging Liliana and Alessia to follow.

"Any ideas how to cast that thing out?" Liliana asked, running alongside him.

"We'll try everything," he answered, breath puffing out.

Dante racked his brain for every spell and chant he'd learned about possession. He had never cast out a malevolent spirit out before, but he would do whatever he could to help them save Fiorella.

As they made it closer to the clearing, he glanced over at Liliana. The light from his spell was too dim now to make out her features, but he could feel the magic rippling off her. She was ready to fight, to do whatever it took to keep her family safe.

"Ometta can't hold her much longer. Liliana, can you cast a holding spell?" he asked.

In answer, Liliana held up her hands and shot out her power. Fiorella's body jerked and lowered to the ground just as Ometta's hold fell.

"Get the others," Dante instructed the little familiar. With a silent nod, she turned away and hobbled toward the villas.

"I can't hold her for long, Dante. She's too strong," Liliana said with a grunt.

"The sleeping tonic! Will that work on her?" Alessia asked, pulling out a vial they'd brought from the shop.

"It's worth a try," Dante said, reaching a hand for it.

Fiorella howled, arms and legs flailing against Liliana's spell.

"Hurry!" Liliana pleaded, voice strained with effort.

Dante uncorked the vial and forced Fiorella's mouth open with an apology. He poured the whole the vial in, wincing as she started choking.

Immediately, she fell quiet, and her body settled. Her eyes closed.

Dante stepped back and looked at Liliana. The light from his spell vanished, leaving them in darkness.

Chapter 18

The Druid

Liliana

L iliana led the way through the dark forest as Dante carried the sleeping Fiorella in his arms. Alessia ran along beside him.

Moonlight trickled in through the treetops as they walked. It was their only light. Having spent her magic to hold Fiorella, Liliana couldn't light their path and Dante's spell had faded.

Though she'd grown up in these woods, everything looked different in the dark. Their once familiar forest had transformed into something entirely foreign on Hallow's Eve. Shadows and wispy white spirits danced in the distance, reveling in their much-awaited freedom. Music drifted from town, the notes taking on an eerie sound as they whistled through the leaves and the branches.

Liliana glanced at Fiorella. Moonlight bathed her sleeping face, highlighting her furrowed brow. Liliana's chest tightened. She should have been looking after her sisters and securing the barriers, not dancing with Dante. Kissing him. She'd let her guard down and now her sister was in trouble.

"Are you sure this is the way?" Alessia asked beside her, pulling her out of her thoughts.

Liliana pushed forward, heart hammering in her ribcage. They were running out of time. Fiorella was running out of time. They couldn't get lost now.

"I—"

A figure appeared ahead of them, cutting her off. It was a boy, not much older than Fiorella. He looked too solid to be a spirit, but there was a white glow coming from him. Something otherworldly.

She took a step toward him, but Dante moved in front of her, blocking her. "Let me go first. Please," he pleaded.

Liliana opened her mouth to object but stopped herself. There was no time to argue.

"Do you know the way to the Fairy gate?" Dante asked the boy.

Large green eyes blinked back at them, half hidden beneath long, tangled brown locks of hair. He stared at Fiorella lying prone in the warlock's arms before looking back at Dante.

"The Fairy gate? Please," Dante's voice echoed through the forest.

The boy shook his head with a frown and pointed toward his ears.

"Oh. You can't hear me," Dante glanced back at Liliana.

She stepped forward and moved her hands in a circle. "The gate," she tried to explain.

Seeming to understand what she was saying, he nodded and waved for them to follow him.

"Are you sure about this?" Alessia whispered to Liliana, grabbing her arm.

Liliana met Dante's gaze. They didn't know who or *what* this boy was. What if he was leading them into a trap?

Dante moved to follow him and threw a look back at them over his shoulder. "It's alright. He's a druid."

Alessia gave Liliana a puzzling look. No time to ponder the new information, Liliana followed Dante and motioned Alessia to catch up.

"How do you know?" Liliana asked Dante, her eyes tracking the strange boy's movements. He slowed his pace for them, steps graceful and purposeful.

"Well, he's not a spirit or fae. He obviously knows this forest well and the voices your sister heard... maybe she is a druid as well."

His words startled Liliana. Could it be true? Druids were similar to witches and warlocks but were self-appointed guardians of nature. They spent their entire lives in the forests and mountains.

They made it to the clearing, the glow of the mushrooms bright in the darkness. Cold air seeped into Liliana's dress and cloak. Alessia huddled beside her, her breath puffing out in little clouds.

Her sister shivered and leaned in to whisper to her. "What does this mean? Has he been here all along? He can't be the voice Fiorella heard before." She glanced back at the boy. "Can he?"

Liliana shook off her questions. "I don't know. None of that matters right now, Alessia. We have to free Fiorella. Then we can figure the rest out."

Alessia nodded, worry swimming in her eyes.

"Alright, Liliana," Dante called her over.

She hurried to his side. He set Fiorella down gently beside the portal and took a step back.

"We're going to try this. Together. Ready?" he held out his hand to Liliana.

She took it, the warmth of his skin sending a ripple of heat through her. Their combined magic pulsed in the air, hot and bright.

"Just repeat the chant after me, alright?"

Liliana nodded. Together, they raised their clasped hands into the air and sent the spell flying to Fiorella. Her body jerked. Liliana repeated Dante's words, her body tight with fear. Pushing the doubt from her mind, she refocused her power.

This would work. This had to work.

Light from the portal burst around them, briefly blinding Liliana. She blinked, trying to adjust her eyes as the light faded.

Fiorella laid still, her eyes closed. Alessia knelt beside her, her gown billowing out behind her. She looked up at Liliana and Dante. "Did it work?"

They exchanged looks. Before Liliana could answer, Fiorella started to stir.

She sat up slowly, a hand to her head and looked around.

"What happened?" she asked, her voice small and strained.

Alessia threw her arms around her with a sob, holding her tight. Liliana's eyes grew hot. Her head pounded and her hands stung, but relief filled her.

Fiorella was okay.

She turned to thank the druid boy, but he was gone. He'd disappeared into the forest.

"Is that it?" Alessia asked softly, looking up at them.

Liliana frowned and glanced at Dante. "That did seem too easy. Are you sure it worked?"

He studied Fiorella's weary looking face and nodded. "I'm pretty sure. There's no evil spirit inside your sister anymore."

"It went back to the portal?" Alessia asked.

Dante looked over at her. "Yes, and we sealed it back up, but we need Massimo to destroy the gate. I don't know about you all, but I would feel much better with this thing destroyed."

"That can wait, though. Can't it? We should get her into the villa," Alessia said, still pressing Fiorella against her chest.

Dante nodded. "I'll carry her back and then return here with Massimo to finish the job."

Liliana's eyes met his. "You've used so much magic already. Don't you need a break first?"

He flashed her a grin. "I still have plenty left. I've always had a lot of stamina."

Unsure how to take his response and too weary to try and rebut, Liliana turned her attention back to her little sister.

"What was that thing that had her?" Alessia whispered with a shudder.

"I don't know, but I'm glad it's gone," Liliana answered.

A chill seeped into her clothes, making her teeth chatter. Pain struck between her eyes, making her rub her forehead. Her body was spent from the spells, but Fiorella was safe. That was what mattered. They were lucky. Lucky that Dante had been there to help.

She glanced at him as he led the way, his back to her. Moonlight filtered through the branches giving them a little light as they walked. The forest had grown strangely quiet, their footsteps echoing loudly in the silence.

Movement behind them caught Liliana's attention. The druid boy? Or were the freed spirits following them? A shiver ran up her spine, making her hurry to catch up with the others.

The sooner they left the eerie forest, the better.

They stood around Fiorella's bed, candles lit all around. Mama, Pamina, and Serafina joined them. The smell of caffé filled the little bedroom. Footsteps echoed from the hall and Liliana turned to see Massimo and Dante. The warlock's eyes met hers with a silent confirmation.

The gate was destroyed.

Massimo entered the room after him and walked over to embrace a teary-eyed Alessia.

Fiorella sat up slowly and looked around. "Where is Tito?" she asked, voice hoarse.

Liliana shared a look with Alessia. The memory of the plant shriveling and collapsing played in her mind.

"Oh, Ella. I'm afraid Tito didn't make it," Alessia answered with a sympathetic look.

Fiorella's eyes watered. She gripped the blanket in her hands and turned to look at Liliana. "I can still save Tito. Bring it back to life. Where—"

"No. You need your rest, *amore*. Tomorrow, we can go look for the plant," Mama stepped in with a firm tone.

Liliana expected her sister to argue or burst into tears. Instead, she just laid back on her pillow and closed her eyes, a small tear running down her face.

Somehow that was worse.

A lump grew in Liliana's throat. She had judged the little plant too harshly. Without it's sacrifice, who knew what would have happened. The spirit could have carried Fiorella far away from them.

Dante's hand touched hers. She looked up at his questioning look. Her heart twisted. She'd misjudged him as well. If he hadn't been there to help...

"I'll look in the forest tomorrow, bring Tito back," Serafina said, interrupting Liliana's thoughts. She leaned forward and squeezed Fiorella's hand. "I'm sorry, Ella. I shouldn't have left you alone. I—" she choked up.

Fiorella gave her a small smile. "It's okay, Fina. I'm okay. Don't be such a crybaby," she added teasingly.

"I want to go with you to find Tito," she said with a determined look.

"You just get some rest. We'll help her find Tito," Pamina said, planting a kiss on Fiorella's forehead.

Mama nodded and ushered them out to the hall. "It's been a long night. I think we should let her sleep. I'll stay with her."

Dante turned to Liliana. "The gate is destroyed, but..." he glanced at her mother, "I think another smothering spell would be wise. I don't know how that creature got past the talisman, but the spirits will be going back at dawn and if word should get out about her power..."

"They won't get her next time," Serafina said with a fierce look.

Liliana nodded in agreement. "We'll be better prepared."

Alessia glanced at Massimo and back to Liliana. "What about that boy?"

"We won't be able to find him until he wants to be found. I don't think he's any threat to Fiorella or any of you," Dante said with a shake of his head.

Weariness filled Liliana. There were so many questions swimming in her head, but her sister was safe for the time being. The gate was destroyed. Zamerra was secured. Hallow's Eve was coming to an end, and she needed to rest.

"Oh, Liliana. The love spell. Is it broken?" Alessia asked, touching her gently on the arm.

Liliana exchanged a look with Dante. "We didn't have time to do it before midnight."

"Does that mean it's permanent now?" Serafina asked.

"Or maybe it's faded on its own?" Pamina asked with an encouraging smile.

"I guess there's only one way to find out," Dante said, deep voice sending a shiver down Liliana's back.

If his presence was still effecting her then the spell must

still be strong. Could he feel it to? The memory of their kiss flitted in Liliana's mind, making her face warm. She'd never been kissed so... thoroughly.

"Liliana?" Alessia's voice drew her back to the present.

Dante was staring at her, an intense look on his face. She avoided his gaze and nodded to the others.

"I'll return to town and wait. We'll see if we're able to stay separate."

She glanced at Fiorella. After what had just happened, she didn't want to leave her sister's side. A shudder went through her at the memory of Fiorella's possession. What would she have done if Dante hadn't been there to help her?

"Oh, no. You can't go down the mountain at this hour. Won't you stay in our guest room?" Mama offered.

Dante smiled politely. "Thank you for your hospitality, Signora, but I do want to get back and make sure everything is set before dawn."

He turned to Liliana and flashed her a smile. "I'll see you later. Unless, of course, the spell is broken. Then... I'll see you again soon?"

The uncertainty in his eyes made Liliana shuffle uncomfortably. She didn't know what to say. If the spell was truly over then there would be no more reason for her to spend another night with the handsome warlock. A slight disappointment filled her at that thought.

Pushing her disappointment aside, she nodded and smiled at him.

"Goodnight then," Dante said softly, his eyes warm.

"Goodnight," Liliana returned just as softly.

Serafina snorted behind them. "How many more times are you two going to say goodnight to each other?"

"Fina," Pamina said with a shake of her head.

She motioned for her to follow her down the hall. Alessia

and Massimo followed. Mama went back into Fiorella's room, leaving them alone.

"I'll walk you back to the wagon," Liliana offered, glancing back at Fiorella's door.

"You don't have to do that. Stay here and get some rest. I assure you, I can find my way back to town," Dante said with a reassuring smile.

Silence stretched between them as Liliana walked with him downstairs. The memory of their kiss replayed in her mind.

Shaking the image away, she looked up at him. "Thank you. For everything. I couldn't have done it without you."

His dark eyes gleamed in the candlelight. "I never expected to hear you say that." His tone was teasing.

Suddenly growing serious, he reached for her hand. "I think we make a pretty good team."

Heat rose up her neck at his touch.

"Sleep well," Dante said giving her a kiss on her hand.

His lips were soft and warm. Catching her breath, Liliana withdrew her hand and watched him leave out the back door.

Standing in the kitchen, she waited to see if the spell would activate. When the pain didn't come, Liliana didn't know whether to be happy or disappointed. Did that mean their bond was broken?

Chapter 19

The Letter

Dante

The back door opened, making Dante bolt up in bed. It was only Ometta, coming in from her hunt. She blinked her large, yellow eyes at him as she flew to her post.

Cold night air swirled in before the door slammed shut. Dante glanced out the window at the moon peeking through the dark clouds. It had been much longer than an hour and still Liliana hadn't come. There was no pain or sign of the spell that had bound them.

They were truly free now. So, why did he feel so awful? As if something was missing.

With a heavy sigh, he leaned back on his pillow and turned his eyes back at the ceiling. It was the first night in a long time he was able to sleep in his own bed. Alone. Yet, he still couldn't sleep. The image of Liliana was burned into his mind. Her dark lashes. Her soft lips. Long, lithe body pressed against his.

A groan escaped him. Now, more than ever, he couldn't get the beautiful witch out of his mind. Was she thinking of him?

The image of her in her bed, remembering their kiss made his skin warm.

Pushing the thoughts away, he chanted a quick sleep spell over himself. She wasn't coming and he needed to rest.

* * *

Dante waved goodbye to his last customer and turned and surveyed the empty shop. The heavy silence and chill of the autumn air filled him with a wistfulness for the Silveri's warm villa and cheerful company. For Liliana.

It had been three days since the masquerade. Funny, they'd been so desperate to break the spell, but now that they were free, Dante missed having her beside him, with her sharp tongue and moody air. The shop felt lonely without her.

Was she missing him too? Why hadn't she come?

Pushing the thoughts away, he made his way back to the kitchen to warm his dinner. The prospect of eating alone was depressing, but he didn't dare eat out that night in case Liliana came.

Business was much steadier now that everyone had heard the story of how he and Liliana had closed the Fairy gate and saved the town. Even Signor Marcello's nasty rumors that they'd been the ones to open the gate in the first place couldn't deter the townsfolk from shopping in Dante's apothecary.

Every time the bell rang, Dante's pulse quickened, and his heart leapt with excitement. Every time it wasn't Liliana, disappointment filled him.

Didn't the way they'd left things unfinished bother her? It bothered *him*.

The bell rang, pulling him out of his thoughts. He walked back to the front and looked up to see the mail courier enter with a friendly wave.

Dante returned his greeting and motioned him toward the counter. The old man hobbled over, pulling out a letter from his satchel. After giving it to Dante and glancing around the store, he took his leave.

Dante held the letter in his hand. It was from Signora Gavella. Opening it quickly, Dante pulled out he paper to read what she'd written.

There was the usual greetings and an apology about the potion and spell. Then, something surprising.

I wouldn't worry too much about the spell. It's only a proximity spell. It should only last for a week or so. It should fade by the time you receive this letter. Maybe even sooner, but definitely before midnight on Hallow's Eve.

The rest of the words blurred together before Dante. Did that mean the spell had already been broken the night of the masquerade? Could that mean that what they'd felt for each other had been real after all?

Dante wasn't sure this revelation would change anything, but he was sure that Liliana would want to know.

Folding the paper into a neat little square and putting it in his pocket, Dante hurried to lock up his shop up. Walking to the back, he stopped suddenly, remembering the gift he'd been wanting to give her.

If she wouldn't come to him, he'd just go to her. Excitement stirred inside him. The kiss had been real. Or at least it had been for him.

The older witch's words rang in his ears.

It will show you your true match.

There would never be any other woman for him. Only Liliana. He just hoped he wasn't too late. That she hadn't rebuilt her barriers to keep him out.

* * *

Dante drove up the mountain, waving to Salvatore and Adriano as he passed by them returning home from town.

The cats and Gio announced his arrival as he pulled up to the Silveri's gate. His stomach fluttered at the prospect of seeing Liliana again. It would be the first time since the masquerade. The memory of their kiss made his pulse quicken.

"Dante!" Fiorella shouted as she and Serafina appeared at the gate.

"It's about time you came to see us," Serafina added, pushing the gate open for him to drive in.

Shooing the cats and Gio out of his path, Serafina and Fiorella moved back.

"How are you two doing?" Dante asked the girls as he hopped down from the wagon.

Serafina unhooked his mare and stroked the horse's face, too busy to pay him any attention.

Fiorella smiled at him. "Good. Why haven't you come to visit?"

"I didn't know I was invited," he answered with a shrug.

He still wasn't sure his arrival would be welcomed by all of them.

Serafina shot him an incredulous look. "Friends are always invited."

Fiorella frowned. "We are friends, aren't we?"

Dante flashed her a wide smile. "Of course! I've been wondering when you would come back to my shop for a visit as well."

Fiorella and Serafina exchanged a look.

"Uh oh. What does that look mean?" Dante asked teasingly.

"Mama said I should stay away from the potions and spells for another week until I'm fully recovered," Fiorella said with an embarrassed smile.

"Ah. That's very wise. Is everyone at home today?" he asked, glancing at the villa.

The girls exchanged another look.

"Oh, yes. She's here," Serafina answered smugly.

"Come on!" Fiorella said, tugging at his arm.

Letting her lead him, Dante followed her toward the back door while Serafina led his horse to a clump of grass where their horse was grazing.

"Look who's here!" Fiorella announced, opening the door for him.

Pamina looked up from the loaf of bread she was slicing. "Hello, Signore," she smiled kindly.

The smell of freshly baked bread and savory soup filled the kitchen. Dante closed the door behind him, walking into the cozy space. A fire blazed from the hearth, heating the room.

"Oh, Signor Lazzaro! Won't you stay for supper?" Liliana's mother asked, waving him to the table.

Dante's gaze darted around the room, feeling a slight disappointment. Where was Liliana?

Realizing she was still waiting on an answer, Dante tipped his hat in response. "That would be lovely. Thank you, Signora Silveri."

The back door opened, and Serafina walked in, stomping the dirt from her boots on the little rug. Bruno, their house elf, peered around Pamina to peek at him.

"Is Liliana home?" Dante asked.

"Dante?" Liliana's voice made him spin.

He turned to find her walking into the kitchen, her mass of curls loose around her face. Surprise was written on her face as she met his gaze. Dante's chest tightened at the sight of her.

"Hello," he said, cursing himself for not thinking of a better opening.

He'd been envisioning this reunion so many times and yet he couldn't think of something better than a pathetic 'hello.'

Her brown eyes met his. "Hello."

Serafina chortled behind them and waved a hand over the bowls Pamina was filling. "Will you two come over here and stop being so awkward? I want to eat."

"Patience, Serafina," Mama spoke up, motioning the girl to her chair.

"I hope you don't mind. Your mother invited me to stay," Dante said, holding Liliana's gaze.

She darted a look to her family and looked back to him. "Oh. Of course."

He held out her chair for her and helped her before taking the open seat next to her. Bruno, overcoming his shyness, sat in the center of the table with his tiny bowl. He held the soup up to his lips like a cup and blew on it, eyeing Dante with curiosity.

"That's Bruno," Fiorella explained as she handed the little elf a small chunk of bread.

He set down his bowl and took the bread greedily, eating it in one bite.

"*Grava fla!*" he demanded in Elvish, holding his hand out for more.

Liliana shook her head and turned to Dante. "Alessia tried teaching him manners, but as you can see that didn't go so well..." her voice trailed off as she met Dante's stare.

Tension hung heavy in the air between them. Dante's heart pounded loudly in his ears and his skin prickled with Liliana's nearness. He wanted to tell her about the letter, but he wanted to do it when they were alone.

"How are things in the shop?" Pamina broke the quiet.

Dante smiled gratefully at her and set his spoon down. "Things are going well. Despite Signor Marcello's rumors, I'm getting a lot business. I could use some help, I think," his gaze darted hopefully to Liliana.

The witch blew on her soup, eyes avoiding his.

Her reaction stung. Irritation filled him. The spell might have forced them together, but he knew the kiss they'd shared hadn't been one-sided. Whether she wanted to admit or not, Liliana had felt something too.

He was sure of it.

"Oh, can't you help him, Liliana?" Fiorella asked with a mouthful of bread.

Liliana shot her a look and glanced over at Dante. "I'm sure he doesn't need my help."

Dante met her unreadable gaze. "Would you come if I asked?"

Everyone fell quiet. Bruno's loud slurping filled the silence.

Eyes on her soup, Liliana shrugged. "Maybe."

Stubborn woman.

Placing a hand on top hers on the table, Dante smiled. She sucked in a breath, head whipping toward his and eyes wide.

Dante's grin widened. So, she did still feel it.

Releasing her hand, he ate his soup and listened as the conversation turned to the upcoming harvest festival and Serafina's birthday. Fiorella told him about the smothering spell they'd performed on her and asked him what would happen when the spell was spent.

Assuring her that he'd be there to help if it was needed, he glanced at Liliana. She'd been quiet during dinner and dessert. Holding her mug up to her lips, she continued ignoring his imploring looks.

It was nearly dark by the time the visit came to an end. Pamina and Signora Silveri started clearing the table and directed the youngest girls to get Dante's horse hitched and ready.

Liliana started to move toward the sink to help her mother. Dante stepped in her path.

Her eyes snapped to his.

"Can I speak with you? Outside maybe?" Dante asked, glancing around at the curious looks on the others faces.

Liliana looked like she was going to object but, at her mother's pointed look, nodded instead. Dante smiled, feeling his stomach flutter.

Serafina and Fiorella raced ahead to get Dante's horse. Cold night air enveloped Dante and Liliana as they walked along the wild garden. Birds flew overhead, calling out noisily, and Gio barked ferociously at them from the safety and warmth of the barn.

"The letter came," Dante said, breaking the silence.

Liliana's head swiveled to him. "The letter? From your mentor?"

He nodded and fished it out of his pocket to hand to her. They paused beside a strange-looking red bush as Liliana read the letter in its entirety. Leaves rustled from the trees surrounding the property, drowning out Gio's incessant barks.

Dante watched Liliana's face as she stared at the letter. A crease appeared in her forehead. Did she realize what the letter meant?

He reached his hand into his pocket and touched the feather delicately. A nervousness filled him. What if she didn't accept his gift? What if she didn't accept him?

"So, the spell faded on its own. Well, I think we already figured that out for ourselves," Liliana's voice interrupted his doubts.

She met his gaze, a slight flush on her face.

"There's something else, too," Dante said, swallowing down his nerves.

Liliana cocked her head. "What is it?"

Touching the feather, Dante chided himself for feeling so nervous. They'd spent so much time together, it wasn't as if she was a stranger. Though there was still so much more that he knew he needed to learn. Like, what kind of music did she like? Where did she like to be touched?

Banishing the images from his mind, he pulled out his gift and presented it to her.

He swallowed hard. "I thought of you."

Her eyes snapped to his. "A feather?"

"It's one of Ometta's. You did say you'd never used magic from a familiar before, didn't you?"

Liliana nodded. "I did."

Dante shrugged. "See? I do remember some things. I'm not completely hopeless." He gave her a lopsided smile.

Liliana stared down at the gift with unreadable expression. "Thank you."

"I know it's not much, but I thought—"

"No. It's... it's perfect. Thank you," she said, eyes meeting his once more.

Silence stretched between them and something completely foreign to Dante enveloped him. A connection—a real one and for once, Dante didn't feel the need to ruin it with a smart remark.

"Happy belated birthday, Liliana."

She smiled.

"Well, I guess I can be serious after all. When it comes to things that are important. Like you. You're important to me, Liliana. I just... wanted you to know that."

"You're... important to me, too."

Dante's grin widened, his pulse quickening at her words. "I can't stop thinking about the masquerade. About the kiss."

Liliana glanced back at her sisters who were waiting beside the wagon with knowing grins. "It was a nice kiss."

Dante stepped closer to her, eyebrow arched. "Just nice?"

She flushed and looked away.

"Should I refresh your memory?" Dante asked, his voice deepening.

Her eyes widened on him. "No! I... I just need some time."

At this, Dante frowned. "You mean even more time than you've already taken trying to avoid me?"

Liliana tucked the feather into her dress and turned away. "I'm not good at... these things."

The vulnerability in her words filled Dante with a surge of protectiveness. Maybe she was letting her walls down after all. Maybe he was too.

"I'm no expert either, but if time is what you need, then I'll give it to you. However, much time you need," his words came out soft.

Liliana nodded in response and started walking toward his wagon.

"Preferably before I'm an old man, though," Dante said with a wink.

Though his tone had lightened, his proclamation was sincere. Liliana was his true match. Of that, he was certain. If only she could accept him.

Chapter 20

True Love

Liliana

L iliana watched him go, her stomach flip-flopping. His words rang in her ears. The letter. The kiss. So, the spell had been broken before the masquerade. That only meant that they'd both chosen to give in. It was physical attraction and nothing more. What he was feeling for her couldn't be deeper than that.

"We're going over to see Alessia and Massimo!" Fiorella exclaimed from behind her.

Liliana nodded her head absent-mindedly at her two sisters. They headed outside the gate in a flurry of skirts and excited squeals.

Wrapping her shawl tighter, Liliana looked up at the near-dark sky. Despite the chill of the air, her skin felt as if it was on fire. Dante's words played over and over again in her mind.

He'd claimed to care about her. As badly as she wanted to believe him, there was still a part of her that was wary. What if it was only a fleeting feeling?

Pushing the thoughts aside, Liliana headed back into the kitchen, her chest aching.

175

Mama looked up from the pile of towels she'd brought in from the clothesline and arched an eyebrow. "Liliana?"

Pamina, who was wiping down the sink, looked up as well. "Where are the girls?"

"They went over to see Alessia and Massimo," Liliana answered, sitting down to help her mother fold the towel.

"And Dante?" Mama pressed.

Liliana shrugged. "He went back to town."

Pamina and Mama exchanged a wary look.

Standing, Mama grabbed the empty basket and glanced at Liliana and Pamina. "I'm going to go out and grab the rest of the clothes and call the girls back too. I'll be back soon."

Nodding in acknowledgement, they watched as she gathered up the basket in her arms, put on her shawl and left out the back.

"Do you want some more caffé?" Pamina asked, breaking the silence.

Liliana nodded. "Thank you."

Pamina handed her the steaming mug and sat down next to her. "You can't ignore him forever, Liliana."

Liliana looked up from the caffé and met her sister's knowing look. "Of course, I can."

"Come on now, surely you're not that proud and stubborn," Pamina said with a frown.

Shrugging, Liliana took a sip from her mug and let the warmth flood through her. Her feelings were complicated. If she were being truthful, she did care for the warlock. Despite her best intentions of hating him, he'd shattered her walls. Left her exposed. It was a feeling she wasn't used to, and she didn't know if she liked it.

Pamina sighed. "I don't understand. At the masquerade, you two seemed... well, don't you care for him?"

The memory of their dance made Liliana pause. His brown

eyes devouring her, ignoring everything else as if she was the only one on the floor. His warm, gentle hands on her hips, holding her possessively close. The smell of his cologne— woodsy and intoxicating. His lips, soft and warm.

"Won't you even give him a chance?" Pamina's gentle voice made her snap out of her memories.

Liliana met her sister's eyes.

"There's still time to make it back to town," Pamina added with a hint.

"To do what? What would I even say?"

Her sister patted her hand and gave her an encouraging smile. "I'm sure it will come to you. Just speak from your heart."

A snort escaped Liliana. Pamina made it sound so easy, but it wasn't. What if she cared more for him than he did for her? What if she opened up, let him in, only to be left heartbroken afterward? He'd made it clear the only true love he had was his magic. Why would she be any different than the other women?

Still....

Despite all the logic swimming in her head, there was still a part of her — a rather big part — that was desperate to give in. To trust him. To trust herself.

Your true match.

Finishing her mug, she set it down loudly on the table and looked at her sister. "I'm probably making the biggest mistake of my life, but... I'm going to go."

Pamina smiled and clapped her hands together excitedly. "To see Dante?"

Liliana nodded and stood. She glanced down at her potion-stained dress and patted her tangled hair. Heat flooded her face. If he could find her attractive in such a state, it had to be real.

"I'll help with your hair," Pamina offered, eyes gleaming with joy.

* * *

This is foolishness.

Liliana held the lantern aloft, making her way down the mountain. Her cloak was enchanted, keeping the cold night air out, but her hands were numb. She'd forgotten her gloves.

She'd forgotten her mind as well, it seemed. What was she thinking? She was nearly tempted to turn back around and go home. Home, where it was warm and safe. Where there was no annoyingly handsome warlock making eyes at her and speaking smooth words.

Pushing the memories away, she focused her attention back on the dirt path ahead. For once, she didn't have a plan. What if Dante wasn't even at home?

The thought worried her. But of course, he would be home. Where else would he be? A giant owl shrieked above, catching her attention. Liliana looked up and smiled. It was Ometta.

The feather Dante had given her had been one of the best gifts she'd ever received. She felt endlessly more powerful, with that new magic now at her fingertips. Excitement filled her at the prospect. She couldn't wait to use it.

Her breath puffed out in front of her as she entered Zamerra. The streetlamps were lit, glowing golden in the night. Smoke rose from the chimneys and all the doors and windows where shuttered closed, giving the town a sleepy look.

Fighting her nerves, Liliana made her way down the cobblestone street to the apothecary. The thought of seeing Dante's surprised face made her quicken her steps.

She glanced around, not seeing anyone else. Though, even if she did, she didn't care. Let them think whatever they wanted. All she cared about was seeing Dante.

When she arrived in front of his shop, the curtain was

closed, and the door locked. Taking a deep breath, Liliana knocked.

Her heart hammered loudly in her ears. What if he didn't answer? She knocked again, louder this time and waited.

Just as she was ready to give up and return home in embarrassment, the door unlocked.

It opened and Dante peered out at her.

"Hello," her voice wavered with uncertainty.

A smile lit up his face when he saw her, making her heart skip.

"Hello," he returned, voice deep, her body suddenly awake with awareness.

Liliana took a deep breath and gestured inside. "May I come in?"

"Well, I'm actually closed, but I think I can make an exception for you," Dante said with a grin.

He opened the door for her and shut it behind her. Shaking off the cold, Liliana looked around the dimly lit shop.

She'd missed the smell of herbs and tonic and the way the colorful glass bottles sparkled in the candlelight. Working alongside Dante hadn't been as awful as she had imagined it would be. In fact, it had been wonderful.

"I was hoping you'd come," Dante said softly, coming to stand beside her.

The seriousness of his tone made her falter. Dante was rarely serious about, well, anything. She turned to look at him. Every word she had rehearsed on the way down was gone. She couldn't think. She could hardly breathe.

Dante held her gaze, a sincerity in his dark eyes that made her stomach flutter. Why had she come again?

"I wanted to say thank you. For my belated birthday present," Liliana said, wincing at the silliness of her words.

Dante's eyebrow arched. "Again?"

She folded her hands together in front of herself. "Yes. It was a lovely gift."

His lips quirked in an amused smile. Stepping closer, he invaded her space, his scent overpowering her senses. The warmth from his body seeped into her skin.

"Liliana, why did you come?" he asked, voice deep and thick.

"Are you going to make me say it?" she asked softly, face heated.

His gaze darkened, flitting to her lips. "Oh, yes. I want to hear you say it."

Her chest tight and body flushed, she turned away to leave. Dante blocked her exit. Looking up at the handsome warlock, she sucked in a breath.

"Tell me why you came. Please," he asked, eyes pleading.

"You'll think it's silly."

"I promise you, I've never been more serious in my entire life," his words echoed around them.

Feeling more exposed than ever, Liliana took a calming breath and met his penetrating gaze.

"The kiss. The dance. The words at the wedding... Did you mean all that?"

His gaze never wavered. "You know I did."

The admission filled Liliana with boldness. If he could be honest and open, then so could she. Maybe they had both changed.

"I meant it, too," she said, hugging herself as she waited for his reply.

He tucked a finger under her chin and lifted her face to meet his. "I mean this one, too."

A thrill ran up her spine as he bent toward her and kissed her softly on the lips.

"And this," he said, planting another kiss against her exposed neck.

She gasped. Heat flooded her. The sensation of his soft lips against her skin made her feel lightheaded. She put her hands out against his chest for support.

At his questioning look, she nodded, unable to speak. Her heart slammed against her ribs as he led her through the kitchen and back to his bedroom. Candles were lit, casting a warm glow against the walls.

Dante helped her out of her cloak and hung it on the bedpost with care. He turned to look at her, the candlelight burning in his eyes. The room smelled like vanilla and wax. Familiar and cozy.

Behind them, his large bed loomed, and silence stretched between them.

"Liliana, I—"

She cut him off with a hand to his lips. "You talk too much," she said softly.

Desire flared in his eyes as he pulled her hand away and drew her against him. His musky smell enveloped her. He covered her lips with his and wrapped his arms around her waist, anchoring her against him.

Liliana parted her lips, giving him entrance. His tongue darted in. A moan escaped her as he deepened the kiss, his body pressing into her.

The back door swung open, making them jump. Liliana turned to see Ometta fly in and hover in the doorway. After one look at the two, she turned around and flew back outside, the door slamming shut after her.

"Are you... sure about this?" Dante asked softly, pulling her attention back.

Liliana shot him a serious look. "Yes."

He led her toward the bed and paused. "This... isn't just a

fleeting romance for me, Liliana. I... want this just as much as you do. I want this to last."

The sincerity in his voice made a lump grow in her throat.

His dark eyes roamed her face. "Is this what you want, too?"

Her heart leapt at his question. Nodding, she reached up to touch his face. "Yes. Now, no more talking."

A smile lit his face. "No more talking," he echoed.

Then he kissed her. Rougher and desperate. Liliana met his kisses with her own desire and need, letting herself give in fully to the moment, to the sensations.

His hands explored her body, eliciting a strangled sound from her as he squeezed and pressed her tighter against him.

Stepping back, Liliana's hands flew to his chest to help him out of his shirt. Her heart hammered loudly in her ears. He threw the discarded garment on the floor and stood before her, glorious.

Liliana sucked in a breath.

She'd envisioned this night since the first time she'd seen him dancing at her sister's wedding. The realization that he'd been waiting for it too made her smile.

Your true match.

The spell had brought them together and, though she still wanted to give the old witch a piece of her mind, she couldn't help but feel grateful. Maybe she'd write a thank you note to her.

Chapter 21

The Next Day

Dante

Dante stifled a groan and looked over at the empty spot beside him. Had Liliana left already? He sat up and glanced at Ometta, who was curled up on her perch, still sleeping.

The memory of the night before made him grin. Before his mind could wander too far, he pushed the heavy covers off and swung his feet off the bed.

Wincing at the cold floor under his bare feet, he made his way to the bathroom. He didn't remember Lilian leaving. A slight disappointment filled him. He'd been hoping to eat breakfast with her. Maybe, a part of him hoped for a repeat of the night before, too.

The sound of dishes clinking together caught his ear. Turning the water off, he opened the door to peer out.

"Liliana?"

"I'm in the kitchen," she called back.

The sound of her voice made his heart skip. So, she hadn't run out on him after all. This filled him with inexplicable joy. If she could change for him, then surely he could change for her.

After dressing himself, he joined her in the kitchen.

"What is this?" he asked as he sat down at the table.

She smiled proudly at him. "I made eggs."

"So, I see. Thank you," he answered, stirring the soupy-looking mixture.

Realizing she was watching and waiting, he spooned a generous helping into his mouth and gave her a nod.

The eggs were runny and over salted but, not wanting to hurt her feelings, he ate them all up.

Liliana made a gagging sound behind him. "These are terrible. Why didn't you say something?"

Dante gave her a sheepish look and shrugged. "I didn't want to spoil the moment."

Cheeks flushed, Liliana sat down beside him and pushed a mug of caffé toward him. "At least this isn't ruined."

She cocked her head and gave him a hopeful smile. "Do you want to have breakfast with me and my family? Pamina makes the best honey cakes."

At this, Dante smiled and nodded. "That sounds wonderful. I think I'll keep the shop closed for today."

"Oh. I'm sorry. I didn't think... you don't have to do that," Liliana said with a frown.

Dante waved her words away. "It's fine. There were no standing appointments today anyway. After last night, I need my rest." He winked at her.

Her face reddened. She sipped her caffé and looked away.

Worry pricked him at her reaction. Laying a gentle hand on her arm, he caught her eye. "No regrets?"

The brilliant smile she gave him made his chest tighten. "No regrets," she agreed.

Both ready, Dante led her to the wagon and cart. The sound of wheels and morning greetings echoed in the distance. All the townsfolk were stirring, getting ready for their day.

Dante helped Liliana into the wagon and took up the reigns. He couldn't think of a better way to spend the day than to be by her side.

Cold air nipped at them as they made their way up the mountain. Puffy, white clouds floated across the blue sky. Dante started humming, glancing over at the smiling witch.

"Must you make that noise?" She asked teasingly.

Dante gave her a wicked smile. "I wasn't the only one making noises last night."

She gave him a flat look and nestled closer against him. The warmth from her body sent a shock of awareness through him. Her lavender soap filled his lungs.

"And what do we tell your family?" he asked, eyebrow raised.

Lilian gave him a side-glance. "We don't have to tell them anything. I'm sure they're aware I wasn't home last night."

Dante chuckled. "No. I mean... about us. Are we courting?"

Liliana frowned. "You never asked to court me."

"Oh, right. I must have missed that step. Will you do me the honors of courting?"

"I... are you being serious?"

"I'm always serious."

She snorted.

Glancing at her, he softened his voice. "I am serious about you, Liliana."

She met his gaze and smiled. "Then, yes."

A tightness filled his chest. Her words both thrilled and terrified him. He'd never made such a serious commitment to anyone else before. What if he did something stupid to ruin it? The last thing he wanted to do was hurt her.

"Wait. Stop here. I want to check the Fairy Gate," Liliana said, glancing at the woods ahead.

Dante frowned. "It's destroyed."

She waved an impatient hand at him. "I know, but I just want to double check."

Shrugging, Dante pulled the cart to the side of the road and offered her a hand down. She took it with a pretty blush, letting him assist her.

He drew her against him and leaned down to kiss her. Her lips were soft and sweet. The sugary taste of her caffè filled his mouth. A groan escaped him as she pulled away.

Before he could kiss her again, she turned on her heel and started walking toward the trees. Dante followed close behind. A cold breeze whipped through the forest, rustling the leaves.

"As much as I love traipsing through these chilly woods, again, I'd much prefer to be inside your villa with some honey cakes and a giant mug of caffè."

Liliana paused and turned to look at him, one eyebrow arched. "Oh? Not back at your shop doing... other things to keep warm?"

Desire flared inside Dante at her heated gaze. He'd like nothing better than to return to what they were doing last night. Her body on top of his. Her curls hanging loose around her, bouncing with each movement.

He groaned. "Liliana, I—"

She cut him off with a wave of her hand. "Shh. What was that?"

Dante frowned and glanced around at the clearing. They'd made it to where the Fairy gate had been. All that was left of the mushrooms was ash. The sulfuric smell of the fire they'd spelled with a drop of Massimo's blood still clung to the air.

"I don't hear anything," Dante said.

Liliana's head whipped toward him. "Maybe if you shut up, you would."

The harshness in her tone startled Dante. What had gotten into her?

She shook her head back and forth and rubbed her forehead with her knuckles.

"Are you alright? What's wrong?" Dante asked, growing concerned.

She stopped rubbing and frowned at him. "Nothing."

Turning away from him, she stared at the remnants of the Fairy gate. Memories from Hallow's Eve flitted into Dante's mind. Their first kiss. The run through the forest. Fiorella's dark laugh.

Maybe Liliana was remembering it too. Heart softening, Dante reached out a hand to touch her shoulder. She startled at his touch and leapt away from him.

"Liliana, what's wrong?"

Her eyes narrowed. "Nothing. I'm fine."

Annoyance rang through Dante at her dismissive tone. Why was she growing closed off again?

"I think you should go," she said, her voice growing softer.

Dante shook his head. "What? Why? I'm not leaving until you tell me what's wrong."

Anger flashed on her face. "I told you. Nothing is wrong. This was a mistake. *You* were a mistake."

Her words cut him through like a knife. *Mistake.*

You are a disappointment. The words of his father rang in his ears, sounding hollow.

"You don't mean that," he said with a slight desperation that made him cringe.

Liliana took a step toward him, chin lifted. "I do. This should never have happened, and you know it too. It was the spell. It—"

"Damn the spell! It was more than that and you know it. Why are you doing this? Is it because you're scared? Scared to be open again? I'm not him, Liliana."

She blinked at him, lips pursed in a thin line. "Go."

Dante took a tentative step closer. "It's okay to be scared. I'm scared too, but what we have... this is real. This is—"

A harsh laugh escaped her, making him pause.

She shook her head at him and gave him a pitying look. "Don't be a fool, Dante. We both knew it wouldn't last. Go before you embarrass yourself more."

The steeliness of her words carved a hollowness inside him. He didn't understand what had changed.

"We both got what we wanted. It's over. Just go," Liliana said with a shrug.

Had it all been a trick? To teach him a lesson? No. Dante refused to believe that. It was more than that.

"Not an hour ago you agreed to a courtship and now you're telling me to go? I think I deserve an explanation. Why are you doing this?"

Liliana scowled at him. "I changed my mind. I don't want this. I never wanted this."

Before he could reply, she turned on her heel and marched away. Dante watched her go, feeling as if she had taken his heart with her.

I never wanted this.

He was at a loss for words. Chasing after her would only make her more defensive. If this was what she truly wanted then he had to let her go. It was the hardest thing he had ever done.

* * *

Back in his shop, Dante paced the wooden floor, trying to replay the sequence of events. Everything had been going so well, what had happened? What changed?

Liliana's words echoed in his ears. *I never wanted this.*

Suddenly, he couldn't stay in the apothecary. Everything

reminded him of Liliana. Memories played in quick succession, making his chest tighten. He didn't know how it had happened so quickly, but she'd become an integral part of his life. How could he pretend as if nothing had happened between them?

A wave of emotion rose inside of him, nearly bringing him to his knees. This wasn't like him. No one had ever had such an effect on him. Was this what love was supposed to feel like?

The image of her cold eyes flashed before him.

Go before you embarrass yourself more. She'd told him.

Go.

So, that's what he would do. He'd leave while he still had some dignity left. It was too late to catch a ride out of Zamerra so he would drive himself to the next town. Stay the night and make travel arrangements in the morning. He couldn't stay there.

Everything reminded him of Liliana and their time together.

True match.

A harsh scoff escaped him, sounding loud in the silence. He'd been wrong. Quelling the dark thoughts, he hurried to the back room to pack the essentials. He wanted to be gone before dawn.

Once packed, Dante cast a locking spell on the shop door and took a look around the abandoned street. Tightness filled his chest. He'd come to think of the little town as home. He would miss it. He would miss Liliana even more.

Pushing her image out of his mind, he led the horse and wagon to the main road. The road that would lead him out of Zamerra. Out of Liliana's life.

Ometta shrieked above him, voicing her disapproval. Well, that was too bad. He was leaving. For how long, he wasn't sure, but he couldn't stay. He just needed some time to sort everything out.

As Dante made it to the edge of town, he glanced back toward the mountain. His heart sank. He had made a promise to Liliana and here he was running away like a coward. If space was what she wanted, then he would give it to her. Maybe it was for the best.

Chapter 22

Missing Warlock

Liliana

"Good morning, Signor Covelli!" Pamina's cheery voice rang in Liliana's ears, grating her nerves.

Liliana had been sensitive and easily irritated all day, though she didn't know why. Everything was setting her on edge.

She turned to see the old baker wave to them as he disappeared into his shop next door. It was nearly lunch time, but Dante's curtain was closed in his shop.

Was he still sleeping?

Her face warmed at the memory of the day before. She had woken in his bed. Then they'd had breakfast or the sorry excuse for breakfast she had made. After that he'd driven her home though she couldn't remember much of the ride.

There were blank spots in her memory, but each time she tried to recall what had happened, her mind drifted to other things. It was as if it didn't want her to remember.

"Did you knock?" Pamina asked, standing behind her.

Liliana shot her a dark look. "Of course."

Pamina's eyes widened at her harsh tone. "I didn't mean to upset you. You've been in such a mood since..."

Liliana silenced her with scowl. Pushing away her irritation, Liliana knocked again and listened. There was no sound coming from the shop.

Pamina frowned. "Maybe he left for the day?"

A grunt escaped Liliana. "I'll go look in the stable."

"I'll do it. You keep knocking," Pamina said, disappearing behind the building.

Liliana sighed heavily, her breath puffing out around her in the chilly air.

Why wasn't he opening? The image of him in bed with Giordana filled her mind, making her seethe. She blinked the image away. What was wrong with her?

Pamina reappeared with a worried look. "I didn't see his horse or his wagon in the stables. Maybe he went out of town?" She said with a shrug.

"With no word to anyone?" Liliana snapped.

Glaring at the door, she lifted her hand to cast a spell.

Pamina gaped at her. "You're not going to—"

She was cut off with the sound of the door unlatching and swinging open. Pamina frowned at her. "Liliana! You can't break into his shop like that."

"Why not?" Liliana shot back, ignoring Pamina's look.

She led the way into the little apothecary. The smell of candlewax and herbs filled her lungs, making her nose itch.

Pamina followed her, shivering in the chilly room. "I don't think he's been here all night."

Liliana's head snapped toward her. "What do you know?"

Hurt flashed across her sister's face. "I wasn't suggesting anything.... I just..."

"Just stop talking! Your voice is so irritating," Liliana said with a huff.

Pamina scowled at her but held her tongue.

Guilt trickled into Liliana' subconscious. It wasn't her sister's fault Dante was gone. Gone with no word, like a thief into the night.

Before her anger could rise, she took a deep breath and looked around the shop. Maybe he'd left a note for her. An explanation. Something. Anything.

Pamina hovered nearby, wringing her hands together in worry. Liliana ignored her as she made her way to the back room.

"Dante?" she called.

Her voice sounded needy and desperate as it echoed around the emptiness. He had better have a good explanation for this disappearance. Heat spread up her neck.

She pushed open the door and glanced at the empty bedroom, unable to bring herself to step inside. Memories flitted before her. His face. His body. His hands on her.

Shutting them away quickly, she turned away and slammed the door shut with a loud 'thud.' She turned on her heel to return to the front room.

"Are you alright?" Pamina asked, forehead scrunched in concern.

Liliana's eyes darted to her. "I will be once I find out where he is." The coldness in her tone surprised her.

Once she found her answers, she'd be able to relax. There had to be a good reason he'd left without a word.

"What are you going to do?" Pamina asked carefully.

Liliana looked around the small kitchen, her gaze snagging on the cauldron. He wouldn't have left his silver cauldron behind if he didn't intend to return for it. None of it made sense.

Why would he leave?

Walking to the cupboard where she knew he kept his maps,

she opened it and pulled the largest one out.

"I'm going to do a locating spell to see where is," she explained at Pamina's questioning look.

She glanced around for the right object to use. Her hand went to her pocket. Ometta's feather. She could use that to locate her and, once she'd located Dante's familiar, she would locate him.

A burning sensation spread through her chest, making her frown. Why did she feel so on edge? Chalking it up to the worry gnawing at her, she pushed away the feeling and pulled the dark feather out.

The memory of him giving it to her made her chest tighten. *I care about you...*

Lies. Pushing away the hurt, she carried it over to his cauldron and turned to grab the rest of the supplies. Thankfully, her sister stayed silent, letting her do her work.

After the ingredients were well-mixed and bubbling, Liliana stood over the cauldron and chanted the spell, letting the magic wash over her.

The feather jerked out of her hand and flew at the map, before burning to ashes.

"What is it? Did you find him?" Pamina asked, almost breathless.

Liliana's jaw clenched. "I found him. He's heading back to the city."

Pamina gaped at her. "The city? Are you sure?"

"Yes," Liliana snapped back.

Eyes wide, Pamina raised her hands in a placating gesture. "Is he okay?"

A harsh laugh escaped Liliana, the sound loud and chilling in the silence.

Pamina frowned and studied her. "Are you... are you okay?"

Without answering, Liliana turned away, brushing the

ashes of the feather to the ground. She headed for the door. Pamina followed.

"Liliana? What are you going to do?"

Liliana's head snapped toward her. "Why don't you go home and make yourself useful in the kitchen? There's something I have to do, and I don't need you slowing me down."

A look of hurt flashed on Pamina's face, making Liliana wince. She hadn't meant to speak so harshly to her.

Taking a deep breath to calm herself, she paused at the doorway. "I'm going after him. He thinks he can just up and run like a coward, I'll—"

"I'm sure he has a good reason for leaving so abruptly. Maybe there was an emergency, and he didn't have time to leave you a note," Pamina cut her off.

Liliana scowled. "You've always been a fool when it comes to men, Pamina. There was no emergency. He got what he wanted and now he thinks he can move on. Well, not without having to face me first."

Pamina's face hardened. "I may be a fool, but you're too quick to judge. Maybe it was your pride that scared him off."

Liliana ignored her, pushing past. Heat rolled through her. Red spots filled her vision and dizziness struck her. She blinked, steadying herself once more. If Dante thought he could run and hide from her, she would show him just how wrong he was.

He never should have messed with her.

Chapter 23

Regrets

Dante

Dante sank miserably into Signora Gavella's worn couch. His head thrummed with pain and his body felt stiff after long nights and days traveling from wagon to coach to wagon. It had taken three days to arrive in Borgo Delle Rose, and each day he wondered if he was making the right choice.

Liliana's face popped into his mind, haunting his every waking and sleeping hour. Guilt filled him at her memory. By now, she would have realized he was gone. What would she think?

That he was a coward, of course. A snort escaped him. She would be right about that. But isn't that what she wanted? She'd told him to go.

"Good morning," Signora Gavella called, entering the room.

She drew the large curtains back, letting the sunlight stream in. Dante winced at the intrusion.

"You can't just lay about for another day, brooding. Go see your friends. Take a walk. Take a bath. Something!" the older witch said, shaking her head at him.

Dante groaned. "I'd rather not."

"Hmm," she said, a hand on her hip.

Dante met her eyes. "What is it? Any sage advice for me?"

Signora Gavella's lips pursed. "Uh-uh. Seeing as you've already done all the scolding and self-loathing, I don't think there's anything left for me to say."

Dante sighed. "Tell me I made the right choice."

Her eyebrow arched. "I think we both know that you didn't."

"I would have only hurt her in the end."

"Like you're hurting her now?"

Dante grunted. "It's for the best. You know how I am. I'm allergic to commitment."

The older witch scoffed. "No. You're afraid of it."

Shaking her head, she pressed a hand atop his. "What is it you're so afraid of, *amore*?"

Dante looked away. "Failing her. Failing everyone."

His father had been right. He was a disappointment.

Her dark eyes narrowed on him. "Running away is just hurting everyone. Including yourself."

"She told me to go."

Signora Gavella sighed. "If it's meant to be, she'll come around. Love always finds a way."

With another shake of her head, the older witch left the room and left him alone in the silence. Dante sighed and rubbed his forehead. He had more than enough regrets to keep him company for the rest of his lonely, miserable life.

Chapter 24

Delle Rose
Liliana

Liliana had never ridden in a coach before. She'd never been in the city before, either. Despite her mother and sister's insistence in accompanying her, she had come alone. This was something she needed to do by herself. It had taken nearly a week to travel and each day she grew angrier at Dante's betrayal.

Anger pulsed hot and bright within her, making her see red. Lately, her emotions had been more heightened than ever. After a quick calming spell, she let the anger fade away. Turning her attention back to the window, she watched as they passed the clustered buildings and statues. Unlike Zamerra, Delle Rose was filled with unending noise.

Wagons and coaches. People shouted to each other in passing. A fresh wave of nerves washed over Liliana as the coachman pulled to a stop. She swallowed hard and grabbed her small sack, holding it tight in her grip. The map was rolled up inside, leading her to Dante.

The door opened and the coachman offered her a hand out. Liliana took it and stepped out, sucking in the cold autumn air.

The city smelled different than Zamerra. Smokier. The clashing smells of savory and sweet filled her lungs and made her stomach roll.

After paying the man and watching him drive off, Liliana ran a gloved hand down her dress and took a steadying breath.

She looked up at the hanging wooden sign above the door. *Signora Gavella's Potion Shop.*

The same woman who had given Dante the love potion. *Your true match.*

At this memory, her skin prickled. It had been false just like the warlock himself. Liliana wasn't his match. There was no match for Dante.

She looked down at her curled fists. What had she expected from him? That he would fall for her as she had for him? That he could feel the same for her as she did for him?

Liliana shook the thought away. Even with the love spell and all they'd been through, it seemed he couldn't commit. Swallowing the lump in her throat, she squared her shoulders and marched up to the door.

She would have an answer from him. Make him look her in the face and tell her why he'd run. Then, she would bury the memory of him once and for all.

An ache spread through her. She wouldn't let him get away with breaking her heart. He would pay.

The shop smelled like mint and roses. An invisible bell chimed as she entered. A few curious faces glanced her way before turning away, too occupied with their own shopping to pay her much mind.

Liliana looked around at the bottles and vials locked behind enchanted glass. Were there more love potions like the one the witch had made for Dante?

"Hello, Signorina! Can I help you find something?" an older woman asked, sidling up her.

Liliana turned to her and frowned. "I'm here to see Dante Lazzaro."

A look of realization crossed the witch's face. Her dark eyes took in Liliana and her lips parted into a sad smile.

"I'm afraid, he doesn't want to see any visitors at the moment," she answered.

A harsh laugh escaped Liliana. "Oh, he doesn't, does he? He will see me."

Signora Gavella's eyebrow arched at Liliana's icy tone. Without a word, she pointed to the staircase in the back. Liliana nodded in response and walked, head held high, upstairs.

The voices of the shoppers faded behind her as she moved forward. A brightly painted yellow door greeted her. The cheery color irritated her. Her skin prickled with anger.

She turned the knob and stormed into the little loft. Her eyes snapped to the dozing warlock on the couch. His long limbs hung over the edge and crumbs covered his shirt. The top buttons were undone, exposing his toned chest.

Liliana cursed herself at the wave of desire that hit her. Even in his crumpled and dirtied clothes, he looked perfect. Dark curls framed his handsome face. His lips were pursed in a pout in his sleep. The memory of those lips on hers sent a ripple of heat across her skin.

He had walked into her life and turned it upside down, made her believe in love, and turned her into a fool. Then, he left. Just like that. As if she had meant nothing to him.

Spots dotted her vision. Without thinking, Liliana raised a hand toward him, ready to cast.

Before she could strike, Dante woke with a start. His brown eyes widened on her. Sitting up, he gaped at her.

"Liliana?"

His deep voice made her flush. She pushed away the feeling. It certainly wasn't the time to let her emotions overpower her.

"Surprised to see me?" she asked, her tone chillier than the air around them.

Dante blinked and rose to his feet, crumbs falling to the ground. "I... what are you doing here?"

Her lips spread into a triumphant smile. "Did you think I wouldn't find you?"

She glanced around at the little room and sneered at him. "I see you've been keeping busy."

"Liliana, I... I'm sorry. I—"

Her bitter laugh cut off his apology. "I'm sorry, too. Sorry you are too much of a coward to say goodbye. Why, Dante? Why did you run?"

His eyes darted away. "I didn't know what to do. I didn't mean to hurt you. I—"

"You didn't hurt me. You think I cared about you? It wasn't real. None of it."

His face hardened. "What do you mean none of it?"

Chest rising and falling quickly, Liliana stepped away from him. "It was lust. That's all. Curiosity."

He frowned at her. "Then why did you come after me?"

She huffed. "Do you think I came to beg for you to come back? I don't care if you come back or stay here. I don't care if I ever see you again. You mean nothing to me. Your father was right about you. You *are* a disappointment."

The words rushed out of her before she could stop them. A sliver of guilt hit her at his wounded look, but she pushed it aside. Despite her words, he had hurt her by leaving. He had hurt her, and she had hurt him. Now, they were even.

Ears ringing, she turned away and marched down the stairs. She ignored everyone's stares as she stormed out. Once outside, dizziness struck her.

Pain speared through her head, making her gasp. What was happening? Before she could stop herself, she collapsed. The world turned dark.

Chapter 25

More Trouble

Dante

After a week staying at Signora Gavella's home, Dante was ready to return to Zamerra. Facing Liliana, on the other hand, was a different story. The words she'd spewed at him in the shop rang in his ears.

You mean nothing to me. Your father was right about you. You are a disappointment.

Pushing away the memory, he threw his scarf around his neck and hurried outside. The street lamps were lit, casting a golden glow on the pebbled streets. Cold bit into his skin as he walked the busy streets toward the station. He would buy his ticket and return to Zamerra. After that, he didn't know what he'd do.

How could he stay in the mountain town after all that had transpired? He knew he'd hurt Liliana despite her adamant denial. The hurt and anger on her face made his chest ached. He had never wanted to hurt her. He should have stayed and confronted her, but it was too late to change the past now.

Dante tucked his hands into his pockets and paused in the

plaza. There was a crowd of people gathered. Musicians played in the center, festive notes floating on the chilly breeze.

It was a love ballad. Once of his favorites though hearing it now only filled him with sadness. He couldn't listen to it without thinking of the beautiful witch and the time that they'd had.

It meant nothing.

Her cold words taunted him. His fingers curled into fists inside his pocket. She couldn't mean that, could she? Their short time together had meant everything to Dante.

Then she'd told him to go and so he did. What else was he supposed to do?

Pushing the thoughts away, he started to turn away from the crowd. A familiar face caught his eyed.

Liliana.

What was she still doing in the city and who was she dancing with? A spark of anger filled him. He watched, jaw tight, as the two danced along with the music. The man's hands moved lower, pulling Liliana tight against him. His lips were pressed to her ear.

Push him away.

To Dante's shock, she only threw her head back and laughed at whatever the man had said. Then her head snapped toward him, a smile spreading on her lips. Something flashed in her eyes. Red. Dark. Inhuman.

Realization struck him. It hadn't been her rejecting him in the woods. Anger rolled through him. He'd been too busy nursing his wounds to realize what had happened. It was the spirit. The one they thought they had banished.

Fear snaked up Dante's spine. Where had Liliana — his Liliana — gone? He strode toward the imposter, his skin growing warm. The spirit had to be very powerful to get through the witch's defenses and go undetected for so long.

This was his fault. If had only realized sooner, he could have freed her.

Striding toward her, Dante ran through all the spells he knew. The one and only casting spell he had performed had been in Zamerra, and that had only been possible with Liliana's help. How was he supposed to do it alone?

"Liliana?" he asked, taking a step closer.

She smiled. "Yes?"

The man she danced with frowned at Dante, but the warlock cut him off with a quick spell. Frozen, the man sputtered in outrage.

Liliana laughed and cocked her head at Dante in amusement.

"Shall we take a walk?" Dante asked, offering her his arm.

She took it and nodded, not giving her dancing partner another glance. Warmth spread through Dante's body at her nearness. His heart raced. He needed to get her away from the crowd. Someplace where he could perform the spell to cast out whatever had entered her.

Nausea filled him. How long had she been controlled by the spirit? How could he have let that happen to her?

"Did you think it would be that easy to get rid of me?" Liliana asked, a flash of red in her eyes.

Dante reeled at the low, gravelly voice coming from Liliana. It was certain now. It was the spirit. The one that had escaped Hallow's Eve and taken over Fiorella.

At his reaction, Liliana's lips spread into a smile. An awful, dark smile.

"You will release her," Dante said, leaning close to her ear.

He gripped her arm tightly in his, walking toward the alley. If he could get her to the shop, he would have more magic at his disposal. He couldn't let her get away. Not with Liliana.

"Isn't this better? It wasn't like she was doing anything worthwhile with her life, anyway."

Dante's eyes narrowed. "Let her go."

She broke out of his grasp and circled him, running a hand down her body, taunting him. "If I let her go, she'll just go back to hating you. Don't be a fool. You'll never have her, but if I stay, I could give you whatever you want."

"I want Liliana back."

She laughed. "Then you'll have to do more than that pitiful spell you tried last time. Give up something. What would you give up to save her?"

Dante's jaw clenched. "Anything."

Her eyebrow arched. "Anything?"

Dante's fingers curled in the air, a spell ready on his fingertips. She continued circling him, dark eyes narrowed in amusement.

"Even what you care about most?" she taunted.

Dante frowned. "I don't know what kind of games you are playing, but I'm no mood for them. Let Liliana go now."

She cackled. "If you want me to let her go then you're going to have to give up your magic. All of it. Forever. That's my price."

His throat dried. Give up his magic? Forever?

"And how do I know you won't go back on our bargain?" He demanded.

Liliana shrugged. "A fae, even as a spirit, can't break a bargain once it's been dealt."

Sucking in a breath, Dante weighed his options. The casting spell hadn't worked. He didn't like the idea of letting the fae spirit loose into the city, but as long as it let Liliana go...

There were enough warlocks and witches who could deal with capturing it and banishing it. He looked down at his hands.

Give up his magic? It was all he had.

"Have you made your choice?" The creature asked, smiling through Liliana.

Dante met its gaze. Though they were the same brown eyes he'd looked into so many times before, there was nothing left of the woman he loved.

Love.

Yes, he realized. He did love her. Even without the love potion. There could be no denying the pull she had on him. Liliana. Her sharp tongue and moody air. Her desperate kisses and soft touch. He loved everything about her.

"Well?" The fae spirit asked, looking out from the eyes of Liliana.

Dante nodded. "Yes. I know what I have to do."

Chapter 26

A New Beginning

Liliana

Liliana woke up with the worst headache she'd ever had. A groan escaped her as she blinked up at the wooden rafters. Home. She was home. How had she gotten there? Pain sliced through her as she tried to remember.

Her throat burned. Images flashed in her mind. A crowd of strangers. Towering buildings. A whispering voice dictating her every move. The fae spirit.

Then, there was Dante. She'd spoken to him, but she couldn't remember what she'd said or rather what the spirit had spoken through her. She saw his brown eyes, so sad then determined. Then there was nothing. What had she done? Panic flared inside her.

Movement caught her eye. She sat up and turned to see a strange creature standing beside her bed. It was oily black with long talons and a forked tail. Large, bright yellow eyes stared out from an oval-shaped head.

"Ometta?" Liliana's voice was breathless.

The familiar only nodded and transformed before her, turning back into the giant owl.

Footsteps sounded outside the door. Liliana looked up to see Alessia burst in, followed by the others. Mama. Pamina. Serafina and Fiorella. Massimo came in last. A lump grew in her throat.

Where was Dante?

"You're finally awake!" Alessia exclaimed, rushing to her side.

Everyone pressed in around her, showering her with hugs and kisses. Their voices blurred together and made Liliana's head pound.

Mama waved for everyone to quiet. Her dark eyes met Liliana's. "How are you feeling, *amore?*"

Pamina handed her a cup of water. Liliana took it with a grateful nod and guzzled it down, letting the cool liquid soothe her throat.

She turned to her mother. "Where is he?"

Mama's eyebrow arched. "Who? Dante?"

"He's at his shop," Serafina answered.

A sigh of relief escaped Liliana. "So, he's okay then?"

Alessia and Pamina exchanged looks, making Liliana frown.

"Well... if you call giving up all his magic for you okay, then I guess so," Serafina said with a snort.

Liliana's gaze snapped to her. "What did you say?"

Her sister shrugged. "He's as magicless as Alessia, now."

Alessia gave her a flat look. "Thank you, Fina."

Serafina shrugged again.

"What happened? I can't remember it all," Liliana said, wincing as the pain sliced through her head again.

Mama moved toward her and stroked the top of her head, lovingly. "There was a fae spirit inside of you," she clucked her tongue. "The same one that had taken hold of Fiorella. I don't know how we missed it."

Fiorella gave her a sympathetic smile.

"If it weren't for Dante, you would have been lost to us," Alessia spoke up, her eyes watery.

Emotion swelled up inside Liliana. She blinked back her own tears, glancing around at the others.

"He gave up his magic to save you," Pamina added with a gentle smile.

"He gave it to you," Massimo spoke up.

Everyone fell quiet. Liliana was speechless. His magic was the most important thing in the world to him. How could he have given it up? She glanced over at Ometta.

His familiar. His magic. He'd given it all up to save her. The words she'd spoken, under the influence of the spirit, replayed in her mind.

Regret washed over her. She couldn't leave things like that. She had to find him. Now.

Throwing the cover off, she swung her legs to the floor.

"What are you going to do?" Serafina asked by the doorway.

Liliana met her gaze. "Give him back his magic."

Fiorella gasped. "How are you going to do that?"

Grabbing her shawl, Liliana draped it around herself. "I don't know, but I'm not going to stop until I do."

Not waiting to answer any more of their questions, she raced down the stairs, Ometta flying behind her.

They hurried outside to the wagon and headed straight for town. Liliana's heart pounded in her ears. Though he'd run, he'd proven himself to her by his sacrifice. No matter what he chose, she had to tell him she was sorry. That she was thankful for his help and that she loved him.

Her heart twisted. Yes, she loved him. Even before the love spell, she had loved him. If he wanted his magic and his freedom, then that was what she would give him. Maybe he couldn't be the man she wanted, but she couldn't let him live the rest of his life without his power.

* * *

Liliana made it to the apothecary in record time. Pushing her nerves aside, she hopped off the wagon and walked up to the door. The curtains were closed, but he had to be home.

"Hello?" she called.

Ometta flew forward and opened the door for her with her magic. No one was home. Disappointment filled Liliana. The idea of seeing Dante again made her stomach flutter. Heading for his kitchen, she breathed in the smell of dried herbs and ash.

Getting to work, she brewed something that would return the warlock's power. Though it was tempting to hold on to his magic, she couldn't do it.

He'd given it all up for her.

If his magic and his freedom were what he truly wanted, she'd give it back up for him. Pushing away the sorrow that this could be it for them, she brushed her curls out of her face and nodded at Ometta.

Liliana was so busy stirring in the last of the ingredients that she didn't notice Dante walk in behind her.

"Um... hello?" His deep voice made her jump.

She turned around to face him, keenly aware of her frizzy hair and ash-stained dress.

His brown eyes were warm and welcoming. An amused smile played on his lips. Liliana's pulse quickened. Even without his magical aura, his presence still had an effect on her.

"Dante," she started, her voice uncertain.

He smiled. "You're awake. Or maybe I'm asleep? You have to tell me if this is a dream. It's only polite."

Liliana shook her head. "You're awake," she said with a slight crack in her voice.

He walked toward her, gaze unwavering. "Are you alright?"

A lump grew in her throat. He'd given up his precious magic to save her and he was asking her if she was okay?

The room seemed to close in on them, the fire warming her through. Behind her, his cauldron bubbled, the sound swallowing up the silence.

"I'm fine," her voice trembled.

He glanced at the brew behind her. "What are you making?"

Liliana followed his gaze. "A potion."

"It's not a love potion, is it?" He teased.

She whipped back to face him. "No. It's a restoration potion. It will restore what's rightfully yours. Hopefully."

A startled look crossed his face. He opened his mouth to object, but she cut him off with a hand to his lips. His soft, warm lips

"Thank you for your sacrifice, Dante, but it's your magic. I'm giving it back. It's what you hold the dearest and you should have it. You worked so hard to achieve it."

He gave her a sad smile. "It can't be undone, Liliana. This sacrifice... it's permanent."

His words rang through her. *Permanent.*

Behind her, the cauldron bubbled, the sound loud in the quiet. He'd given up the very thing he loved most to save her. Her throat grew scratchy. She didn't know what to say. Despite the anger she'd felt after his leave, she was touched that he'd given up his magic for her.

"I'm sorry for leaving," Dante said softly.

Liliana met his gaze. His eyes roamed over her face, making her skin heat. The sincerity she saw there made her chest ache.

"I should have known it wasn't you telling me to go," he added with a grunt.

Liliana frowned. "I told you to go?"

His eyes met hers. "In the forest. I should have known it was the spirit speaking. Not you. I'm sorry."

Anger boiled inside her. A part of her longed to hunt down the spirit herself and get revenge for the mess it had left her in. She would demand it give Dante's magic back to him. It might take years to find and capture the creature, but it could be done. Though if what Dante said was true, then there would be nothing that could undo his sacrifice.

Pushing the sad thoughts away, she nodded. "I'm sorry too. For what I said. In the city, I mean. Well, for all of it. When it came down to it, you were there, Dante. For my sister, and also for me. I'll be forever grateful for your bravery and strength."

The warlock scoffed. "You are much braver than I am. I ran because I was scared. It was a mistake. One I'll regret making every day, but giving up my magic to bring you back, I don't regret that."

Liliana's eyes grew hot. She'd always wondered what it would be like to have more magic. More power and possibilities. Though she never imagined it would be at the expense of Dante losing his. It didn't seem fair. Life, though, was hardly ever fair.

"Thank you. I... what is going to happen now with your shop?"

Dante shrugged. "Maybe you would be interested in running it? You are the best potion maker in town."

"You wouldn't have to work with me," he added quietly.

Liliana's eyes snapped to his. Was he leaving again? The thought sent a spear of pain through her.

"I would understand if you never wanted to see me again after I ran like a coward."

Liliana shook her head. "No. This is your shop. We are partners, remember?"

A smile spread on Dante's face. "Yes. Partners. I think we make a pretty good team."

Liliana's heart flip-flopped. The words from the love spell played in her mind.

True match.

She took a deep breath and nodded. "I think so too."

They fell quiet. The bubbling in the cauldron and the sound of wagon wheels and people chattering outside filled the silence.

Dante's dark eyes studied her, a troubled look on his face. Heart swelling with a mix of emotions, Liliana looked away and smoothed down her dress.

"Well, I better get back to the villa. There's much to do before the Harvest Festival."

Dante frowned but didn't try to stop her. He followed her outside the shop and stopped in the doorway.

"Goodbye, Dante," Liliana said softly, turning to walk toward the wagon.

Her eyes grew hot as she walked away. It wasn't really goodbye, but he hadn't stopped her. They'd gone through so much together, Liliana wasn't sure how they could start over. Pretend as if all those things hadn't happened. But for him, she would try.

Chapter 27

Happy Ever After
Dante

This was it. Dante knew if he let her go now, he'd never forgive himself. She was his true match in every way and there would never be anyone else for him.

The memory of her kiss, her touch, came flooding back to him. No matter what he did, he would always think of her. She was forever branded on his heart.

He watched as she slipped into the crowd, her dark curls disappearing. Once she was gone it would be too late.

"Wait!" he called, chasing after her.

She turned back to him, her dark eyes hopeful and unsure. Dante hated that he'd put that uncertainty there. That he'd let her down. He'd spend the rest of his life striving to make it up to her. If she would have him.

"Liliana, I... I know I've already apologized, and there's nothing I can say to undo the hurt I've caused you. It will probably take a long time before you trust me again. That is, if you ever do, but I hope that you can give me another chance."

He took a deep breath. "I promise I'll never run again. You mean more to me than... anything."

"Anything?" she asked, eyebrow raised.

Dante nodded in earnest and reached for her hand. "Yes."

"Even your magic?" Her tone was light, but her eyes were serious.

He lifted her hand to his lips and planted a soft kiss on it. "Much more. I'd give my magic up all over again if it meant we could be together."

She glanced down at her hand where he'd kissed her. "I would never ask you to do that."

A smile twisted his lips. The sincerity and warmth in her tone gave him hope. Hope that maybe all wasn't lost.

"Will you give me another chance? I can't guarantee I'll get things right all the time, but I can promise I'll keep trying. Until my last breath."

Liliana's face was downcast, her arms wrapped tightly around herself.

Dante's throat swelled with emotion and an aching spread through his chest as he waited for her answer. He didn't know what he'd do if she rejected him now.

The crowd moved around them, oblivious to their situation. Wagon wheels against cobblestone echoed along with cheerful voices. Everyone continued on with their busy lives, but Dante couldn't move. Not until he heard her response.

"I love you, Liliana. Only you. Always you," Dante said, reaching out to touch her.

He cupped her jaw gently, lifting her face to meet his.

Her warm brown eyes stared back at him. "I love you, too," she said softly.

Dante couldn't stop the smile spreading on his face. His heart leapt with excitement and hope.

She loved him!

"Does this mean you'll give me another chance?" He asked, sounding breathless.

Her lips parted into a brilliant smile. "Well, since you asked so nicely."

Dante felt the urge to kiss her. He bent his face to hers, breathing in her sweet smell. She tilted her head up to meet his. Heat spread through Dante at the contact. Her lips were soft and warm, tasting like sugar and caffé.

"There you are!" A voice interrupted them.

With a groan, he pulled away, ending the kiss much too quickly. The dazed look in Liliana's eyes matched his own feelings.

Dante would never get tired of kissing her.

Shaking away the thoughts, he turned to see Fiorella and Serafina heading toward them with eager faces.

"I did it! I revived Tito. Come see!" Fiorella said with an excited squeal as she hugged her sister.

She motioned for them to follow her back to their wagon, where their mother waited. Dante glanced at Liliana.

She shrugged at him, still smiling. "You don't have to come if you don't want to."

A scoff escaped him. "Don't be silly. Of course, I want to come. I wouldn't miss it for anything."

He offered her his arm and walked toward the wagon. "I don't want to miss one moment with you."

She smiled, dark eyes gleaming with delight. "Even the borings ones?"

Dante paused to help her into the wagon and glanced at the others waiting. "With your family? I don't believe there will be any boring moments."

Liliana snorted and threw him a wry look. "With Hallow's Eve over, I'm afraid Zamerra isn't quite as exciting. It's nothing like the city."

"Oh, but don't forget the Harvest Festival!" Fiorella spoke up, waving at them to hurry.

Dante climbed into the back of the wagon cart and sat himself next to Liliana. "Harvest Festival?" he asked.

She rested her head against his shoulders. "More eating and dancing, but without any spirits to worry about."

Dante kissed the top of her head. "Oh, I do like eating and dancing."

Serafina snorted across from them, bracing her hand on the edge of the cart as they started moving.

"Pamina makes the best pies! Wait until you taste her pumpkin pie," Fiorella said from the driver's bench behind them.

"That sounds delicious, but I prefer her honey cakes," Dante replied with a raised brow.

Liliana patted his hand lovingly and gave him an innocent smile. "Yes. We all know how you love your honey cakes. I'm sure she'll make some extra for you."

He wrapped an arm around her shoulders as the wagon rolled slowly. Soon, the noise of town faded away and the sound of the wagon wheels against the dirt and leaves filled the silence. Serafina sat across from them, looking up at the flock of birds soaring against the clear sky.

Behind them, Signora Silveri and Fiorella chattered about the upcoming festival, their voices rising over the sound of the wheels.

Dante glanced down at Liliana and smiled. "So, this is love, huh?"

She met his eyes and returned his smile. "Yes. This is love."

His grin widened. For once, there was nothing left to say.

The End

Epilogue

Liliana

W ood crackled in the fireplace as Liliana sipped caffé from her mug. She sat curled on her family's worn, lumpy sofa, next to her handsome fiancé. He glanced over at her, dark eyes full of promise, and a small smile on his lips. Lips that would soon be on hers once they left for home.

"Did you hear the news? Signor Covelli died in his sleep," Serafina said, interrupting her thoughts.

Liliana turned to her and back to the conversation.

Pamina nodded with a sad smile. "He always had a kind word to say about my pies."

"Oh. No, I hadn't heard," Liliana said, glancing at Dante.

The warlock frowned. "Me neither. That's a pity. What's going to happen to his shop now?"

"I assume it will pass on to his nearest relative," Mama answered from her recliner.

"Who is his nearest relative? I didn't think he had any family nearby," Alessia said, looking to Massimo.

The fae count shrugged. "I don't believe he does. But if

219

there's no one to claim it, it will become property of the town. I'm sure someone else will buy it."

Pamina frowned. "How sad. Can you imagine living and dying all alone like that? I should have spent more time befriending him."

"Maybe you can purchase the bakery yourself. I'm sure the late Signore would approve of that," Dante spoke up, giving Pamina an encouraging smile.

"Oh! I can help you run the bakery," Fiorella said excitedly, looking up from her sketchbook.

Pamina shook her head. "I wouldn't know the first thing about running a bakery. Besides, I'm sure he must have someone in his family who would be a good fit for that."

"Besides, you should be spending time practicing your magic, Ella," Alessia said, giving Fiorella a pointed look.

Fiorella glanced up from her drawing and looked over at Tito, who stood beside her in a giant pot. "I have been practicing. I practice every day."

Mama nodded in agreement. "And you've been doing wonderfully, *amore*."

Liliana exchanged a look with Pamina. Now that Pamina was the oldest still at home, she would be the first to notice any changes in Fiorella's magic. The smothering spell they'd placed would only hold for so long before their sister's power broke free. Thankfully, they had time before that happened. Time to find something that would help.

Liliana hated the thought of her sister forced to wear the enchanted gloves for the rest of her life. Without control of her magic, what kind of future could the young witch have?

As Liliana glanced around at their growing family, a warmth spread through her. Mama was right. Things were changing for the better in Zamerra. With those changes, she hoped for bright futures for all of them.

"Are you going to eat that?" Dante's deep voice interrupted her musings.

She glanced up to see him eyeing her plate eagerly. With an affectionate snort, she picked up the sticky honey cake and held it up to his lips.

Dark eyebrow arched, Dante leaned forward and ate if from her fingers, eyes gleaming.

Heat rushed across Liliana's face. She hadn't known the simple act would be so... arousing.

Massimo cleared his throat uncomfortably, drawing their attention back to the others. Mama, Alessia and Pamina smiled at them, but the younger girls were too preoccupied feeding Tito bits of pastry to notice.

"Have you set a date for the wedding yet?" Pamina asked, eyes wistful.

Liliana and Dante exchanged looks.

"We were thinking right before the yuletide," Liliana answered for them both.

Mama clapped her hands excitedly. "Oh, lovely! That's the perfect birthday present for me."

Pamina nodded in agreement. "A winter wedding! That will be so beautiful."

At this, Serafina and Fiorella turned to them in unison.

"Ooh! A winter wedding!"

"I hope there's snow!" Fiorella exclaimed dreamily.

Alessia smiled too and squeezed Liliana's hand. "We'll help with everything. Anything you need. It's going to be lovely. I'm so happy for you. For both of you," she added, glancing at Dante.

Liliana followed her gaze and smiled up at her fiancé. "I guess we can't go through with the elopement after all."

Dante winked at her. "I'll marry you in any way or fashion, you'd like, Liliana."

He stood and stretched his legs. "As lovely as this evening has been, I'm afraid we must take our leave. It's been a long day and we're tired. It is getting rather late as well..."

Fiorella frowned. "No, it's not. How can you be tired already after the caffè?"

Liliana shot her fiancé a pointed look and turned to her family. "It has been a long day. We'll see you all in the morning."

Massimo and Alessia exchanged knowing looks while the others voiced their goodbyes. After many hugs and promises to return, they made their way outside to the wagon. Serafina silenced the cats and Gio for them as they hitched their horse and cart.

"Goodnight!" Liliana called once again as they drove through the gate.

Above them the sun was setting, painting the sky a brilliant orange-red. Cold air enveloped them, making Liliana snuggle closer to Dante.

"Tired, huh?" She asked in a teasing tone.

He gave her a side-eyed glance and grinned. "Not yet, but I plan to be."

Liliana flushed at his suggestive tone. As much as she loved spending time with her family, it was nice to have time alone with Dante.

The wagon wheels against the dirt path swallowed up the silence. Liliana sank lower onto the bench, resting her head against Dante's shoulder. His body warmed her.

He started humming his favorite ballad, the sound reverberating through Liliana. She smiled at the off-key notes and hummed along.

Leaning over, he pressed a kiss to her forehead. Liliana looked up and met his smoldering gaze. Feeling bold, she pulled his face closer and kissed him.

Heat rushed through her at the contact. His lips were soft and tasted like caffé and honey. The wagon jerked, pulling them apart.

Dante yanked the reins, guiding the horse and cart back to the center of the road.

Liliana shook her head at him. "You better pay attention to driving or we'll end up off the mountain."

He glanced over at her. "Then you better stop distracting me. Though, I promise you, if we end up as spirits, I'll make sure we spend eternity together in the most pleasurable, enviable bliss."

A shiver went up her spine at his deep, rough voice.

Liliana smiled. *Eternity together.* That was a promise she knew he would keep. *They* would keep.

Thank you for reading! Pamina's story comes next in *The Goblin's Bride*. You can also read Alessia and Massimo's story in *The Fae's Bride*. Each book features a different sister and some of the same characters as well as new ones.

Acknowledgments

A big thank you to my husband who made this cover and the cover for book one. There were many late nights spent in Photoshop tweaking and tweaking.

A huge thank you to my editor Letizia Secco who helped me in a pinch when my regular editor was booked. Your input was invaluable. Especially with the Italian!

I also want to thank my editor at Cate Edits for working with me on the overall series and characters.

Finally a big thank you to YOU for reading this story. If you enjoyed it, please consider leaving a review.

Thank you!

Also by R. L. Medina

The Silveri Sisters Series

Book 1: The Fae's Bride

Book 2: The Warlock's Bride

Book 3: The Goblin's Bride

Book 4: The Wolf's Bride

Book 5: The Druid's Bride

YA Fantasy

The Inner World Series

Prequel: Feylin

Book 1: Princess of the Elves

Book 2: Goblin King

Book 3: Fae War

Sign up at my website for a FREE Short story

GRIMM Academy Series

Book 1: Shifters and Secrets

Book 2: Vampires and Werewolves

Book 3: Witches and Wizards

Blood Moon Covenant Series

Book 1: Order

Coming soon...

Book 2: Allegiance

Book 3: Betrayal

About the Author

R. L. Medina is a Bolivian American Fantasy author. At age six, she vowed to hate reading forever. That hate quickly turned to love (or obsession) and by age eight she was filling every notebook with story after story. Now she juggles her time between a busy seven year old and all the characters that demand her time. When she's not exploring all the Sci-fi/Fantasy worlds in her head, she enjoys life with her family in Florida.

Check out her website at www.rlmedina.com for a free story, giveaways, and updates!

You can also find her embarrassing herself on TikTok @bookdragonlife and the social media channels below:

Printed in Great Britain
by Amazon

58954125R00136